Wakefield Press

On Edge

T0359668

On Edge

edited by

Christy Di Frances
Susan Errington
Rachel Hennessy
Emmett Stinson

Wakefield Press

Wakefield Press
1 The Parade West
Kent Town
South Australia 5067
www.wakefieldpress.com.au

First published 2005

Cover by Slinc Creative
Text design by Clinton Ellicott, Wakefield Press
Typeset by Ryan Paine, Wakefield Press
Printed and bound by Hyde Park Press

National Library of Australia
Cataloguing-in-publication entry

On edge.

ISBN 1 86254 691 6.

1. Short stories, Australian. 2. Australian poetry – 21st century.
3. Australian poetry – South Australia. I. Di Frances, Christy.

A820.8099423

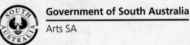

Contents

Introduction

Professor of Creative Writing, The University of Adelaide

Not everyone can see the ghost that walks the times, but it's there, in the shadows, around the corner, under cover of dark, in our dreams. It's the mysterious figure that pops up on the pathway, warns us or beckons us, hinting at what's really going on. It's the hidden shape of things, the form of our desires and fears, the surprising, disturbing meaning of our world. Writers know that ghost. As they write of their discontents or give voice to their contentments, their words give line and body to the tricky, terrifying spirit of the age. Their imaginations follow courageously when cracks open in the surface of things, along the edge of the unknown, until something is glimpsed. Their stories bring the new, the old – the *Zeitgeist* – back home to us, and the skin on the back of the neck bristles.

In *On Edge*, twenty-five writers catch our times in their creative words. They go into the dark to write of loss, violence, abandonment, self-harm, the eruption of demons and the play of the occult. They return to the light with humour, renewal and the appreciation of time's gifts. They write of relationships, broken or reaffirmed, between lovers, partners, parents and children. They speculate *behind shades*. They fantasise the *reasons for green* or black or white. They divine the depths of place and situation, seeking out *rarity* and valuing *the unparallelled*. Patsy Cline's tears, a sixth toe in a glass vial, a possum dead in its tracks, ripe figs falling to earth, sound that is silent.

On Edge is written and edited by writers associated with the University of Adelaide. It builds on the acclaimed series of anthologies published in previous years through successful creative partnership between Wakefield Press and the University of Adelaide.

The series includes work by writers with established literary reputations, emergent writers who have gone on to publish major work, and writers who are fresh to print, free to experiment and find themselves. Craft is a double-edged word; it is the tough discipline a writer spends a lifetime learning, but it is also the magic that enables a writer to bring feelings and visions to life, as if from thin air. This year's anthology, full of strong, edgy, probing pieces, shows the writer's craft at full stretch, giving powerful and pleasurable expression to our troubled times.

Day #41

Stefan Laszczuk

I woke up hungover and hungry. There was no food in the fridge so I got on my bike and went looking for somewhere to eat. I rode all the way down a very steep hill. I went so fast my eyes started watering. When I got to the bottom, the first place I saw was a Hungry Jack's. I hate that place. I don't know why I went in, but I did. I was just kind of switched off, I guess. On autopilot, unable to stop myself from crashing into a mountain of grease, fat and sugar.

I took my 'food' from an ugly girl with a lisp, grabbed a complimentary newspaper and sat down. Looked around. There were three other men in the restaurant sitting down on their own and eating crap and reading newspapers. They looked like lonely losers. And there were a couple of families. Kids screaming and running around everywhere. A girl was standing, holding open the door to the playground. She was screaming the loudest. 'Mummy! Muuuuu-mmmmmmmmy!!!! MUUUUUUU-MMYYYY!!!!!!!!!'

I hate screaming kids. I looked around again at the three losers sitting on their own eating and reading. Apart from the fact that I couldn't deal with all the noise around me, I couldn't deal with the fact that if I took a bite of the greasy piece of crap in front of me, I would become lonely loser number four, so I left the 'food' on my tray untouched and I left my newspaper and I went outside and got back on my bike.

I had to ride back up the very steep hill to get home. It's no fun riding up hills hungover. My chest hurt. And the passing trucks somehow seemed ten times as loud and threatening. I started thinking one of them was finally going to clean me up. Suck me under the tyres and squeeze my fucking brains out all over the road.

Snap my bones between the double-wheels and crunch and crack me like a fucking lobster. Then two weeks later all that would be left of me would be a stain on the road and perhaps one of my bloodied sneakers lost somewhere in the roadside undergrowth.

But I got to the top without being wasted by a truck, and pulled over to take a break and a swig of cool water from the bottle in my rucksack. I was panting and sweating and my lungs hurt as I looked back on the city below me. I suddenly yelled out 'Fuck you!' without really meaning to. I sounded angry. I didn't like sounding angry so I tried to re-yell it, and to sound sort of triumphant instead. It didn't work. There was no self-belief in my voice. I wondered briefly whether I was shouting at you or at the city. But I'd never shouted at you so it must have been the city.

When I got home I had a shower. The water pressure has been slowly getting worse over the last week. I had to turn the hot on full just to get a trickle. I bent forward under the trickle and let it run down the back of my neck and down my back. The shower floor was dirty. It felt kind of greasy and there was some sort of blue fluff everywhere. Like fluff from a towel – only I knew it wasn't fluff from a towel. I didn't own any towels that were fluffy. I used my toes to drag the fluff in from all parts of the cubicle floor and tried to push it towards the drain. The trickle of water running down my neck and my back was in no way powerful enough to sweep the fluff down the drain. I had to keep prodding and poking it down the drain holes with my toes. As I rolled my toes back and forth over the drain I happened to dislodge some hair that had gathered there. I leant down to pick it out of the drain, to make room for the fluff. It was a clump of your long hairs. I dropped them back to the shower floor and stood up and turned off the trickle and dried myself. Then I took your clump of hairs off the shower floor and went to the kitchen and put it in the bin.

I was still hungry so after I got dressed again, I tried to walk to the shops to get some food. I walked up to the end of the road and back again three times before I could bring myself to keep walking to the shops. It took me three times because at the shops there's this friendly redhead who works on Mondays and I just knew if I went shopping that I was going to have to deal with her friendly inquiry into whether I had a good weekend or not. I wasn't in the mood for dealing with friendly inquiries. Just the thought of engaging in small talk made me feel like I was going to flip out. That's why I kept turning around at the end of my street and coming back. Then, on the third time, I realised that I was shaking and that I would have to eat at some point or I would faint, so I kept going.

When I got to the supermarket I picked up a steak and a light globe. The queue for the express lane was pretty bad. I had to stand there at least three minutes before it moved once. The noise of the place was making me nervous. My head felt like it had been cracked open and become some kind of vacuum cleaner/black hole that sucked in all the bullshit supermarket sounds. People talking. Cash registers beeping. Kids screaming again (fucking kids, I tell you – always with the screaming).

'Crunchy Granola' was playing on the radio. I looked at the checkout people behind the counter. They all seemed in a good mood, especially the redhead. I was dreading a friendly weekend inquiry. I wondered whether I could handle it. Or whether I'd flip out and scream and walk over and start smashing my head on the linoleum counter. What would happen if I did? Would I knock myself out? Would they call an ambulance? Would I be able to come back one day and shop at the supermarket again? Would all the supermarket staff whisper about me every time I came in, saying that I was the guy who smashed his own head on the super-market counter?

I was standing between some old bloke buying a pair of rubber gloves and a fat guy in a suit. I recognised the fat guy in the suit. I'd seen him once in a courthouse when I went to watch some trials because I was bored. He had been caught shoplifting lady's under-wear. His excuse to the judge was that he had forgotten to buy his wife a Valentine's Day present and so he decided to steal it. It was a stupid, thoughtless act, he admitted. The judge agreed it was stupid, especially considering he had been busted mid-June. 'That's some sort of late Valentine,' he had said.

'Yes, Your Honour,' the fat guy had replied and I knew I'd never forget the look on his face.

'Crunchy Granola' finished on the radio. Thank God. The fat guy reached behind him to give his arse crack a quick scratch and adjust his underwear through his trousers. I wondered whether he was wearing a pair of women's panties.

There were three girls serving in the express lane. The friendly redhead was there. There was also a blonde and a brunette. I had a one in three chance of being served by the redhead. I crossed my fingers. Fuck. Make that one in two. The fat guy stepped forward to be served by the blonde. It was touch and go who would finish serving their customer first out of the red-haired girl and the brunette. The redhead won by a nose. She seemed to bag groceries extra fast whenever she saw me next in line. I shuffled forward and put my stuff on her counter.

'Hello there,' she said.

'Hello.'

'So how was your weekend?' She smiled. 'Did you get up to no good?' She gave me a knowing wink.

I looked down at the counter. The linoleum was green and white interlocking flowery sort of patterns. There was a little metal rim running around the edge, held fast by what looked to be rusty nails. There was one nail sticking out a bit. It had a loop of fishing wire wrapped around it. The fishing wire was attached to a netted pack of Freddo Frogs. Peppermint flavour. The frogs were selling for 65 cents each. I looked up at the girl.

'Yeah,' I said. 'No good.'

She kept smiling as she scanned my items. The light globe and the hunk of steak.

'Steak for tea tonight, then?' she said as I handed her a twenty.

'No, actually I'm eating the light globe for tea.'

She giggled and gave me my change. I noticed that she'd accidentally short-changed me. I didn't bother pointing it out. I just got the fuck out of there.

As I was walking home I toyed with the idea of eating the light globe. Wondered what would happen. It would cut the hell out of my mouth, that was for sure. I wondered whether I would lose my tongue. Whether shards of glass would stick in my teeth, whether, if I swallowed it, the shards of glass would run down my throat and slice me up from the inside. If it would cut my stomach to shreds and make me start pissing and shitting blood. I decided to have the steak.

When I got home I cooked the steak with some vegies I had in the fridge. Potatoes. Carrots. Broccoli. Topped it all with a garlic and soy cream sauce. I made that dish for you once. You hardly touched it. You just smiled politely and told me you weren't very hungry. Up until that point I had been very proud of how nice that meal had always tasted but it hasn't ever tasted quite as nice since. I still eat it though cause I don't know how to cook much else.

When I'd eaten what I could and scraped the rest into the bin, I took the garbage out and then had a cigarette. It was my first cigarette for the day and it was my last. When I stubbed out the cigarette I went back inside and sat in front of the TV for about seven hours without really watching anything. Eventually I decided to go to bed cause I could barely keep my eyes open. So I went to my room and I undressed and pulled back the covers. I noticed that the sheets could do with a wash. I got into bed and lay there in the dark for a while and thought about jerking off, but I couldn't cause I just kept thinking of you. And about the fact that you were gone and that you weren't coming back.

No Epic Here

A M Sladdin

After all
I can fold
our 15 missing years
almost as small
as a Haiku
What I knew of him
All that he wanted of me

My Friend Jim

Dominique Wilson

My friend Jim rang me last night. He said Sister Susie Singleton took him for a walk around the grounds and the trees were on fire but she put the fire out. He said he didn't know before if Sister Singleton was a saint or sinner, but now he knows she's a saint because she put out the fires. He said they had lamb stew for dinner that night, then he went to bed early and Sister Singleton checked his room to make sure he was safe.

My friend Jim rang me last night. He said he painted a picture of his garden back home. Sister Susie said she liked it but they heard her and messed it all up when his back was turned and Sister Susie was sad and he got mad. But Sister Susie gave him a drink and checked his room and he slept such a long time he missed breakfast and lunch. He said he wanted to throw out his painting but when he got there it was all fixed again. He thinks Sister Susie must have done it for him and although she said no he knows that she did.

My friend Jim rang me last night. He said there's a new guy living there now and he thinks *he* may be one of them. He said Sister Susie took *him* for a walk and when he asked to go too she said no. He said they had meat pie for dinner that night but he didn't eat any. He was thinking instead.

My friend Jim rang me last night. He said his sister was dead but I mustn't tell because it's a secret and no one must know. He said they had chocolates as a special treat after lunch and maybe next week they'll get cream cakes instead. He said he didn't have any because he saw their mark on one, and he told Sister Susie, but she said don't be so silly, I bought these myself. In the afternoon she played Scrabble with him and when he won the game she told him she was proud.

My friend Jim rang me last night. He said he'd seen them standing there in his room and they told him they knew all about his secret. He said they told him I was the one who told and why did I do that when I say I'm his friend? He said he called Sister Susie but she didn't come. Instead she sent another who wouldn't drive them away.

My friend Jim rang me last night. He said that bitch Susanne was giving him hell. He said he'd worked out all about her and maybe me too so I'd better watch out. He said he knew which ones of us were with them but he was too smart and we couldn't get him now even if we tried. He said it was no use burning down the grounds because he'd built a shelter that no one had found. He said they were talking of stopping him phoning but he had his ways and they couldn't always watch him.

My friend Jim rang me last night. He said that Sister slut had tried to get into his sleep but he was too smart and had kicked her and punched her. He said she had started to snap and to snarl and he smelled the hot sulphur but someone heard and came in. He said they had kept him in a stinking solitary room on his own and wouldn't let him out which is why he hadn't called.

My friend Jim rang me last night. He said that sorceress slut Singleton slithered sensually surrounding secondary sleepers and spewed subliminal smut. He said slobbering scarlet sows screeched sublime satanic symphonies and sapropelic scavengers sucked subcutaneous suppurations and shimmering shrivelled saffron spiders spun silken sarcophagi while spurning Satyrs swiftly snared succourless souls.

My friend Jim rang me last night. He said Sister Singleton sat with him all night, and when they came again she'd scattered them all. He said he saw the singed branches on the trees outside his window, and wanted to go out and heal them, but they stopped him for now. He said he saw sparrows building nests under the eaves, and he hoped the coming spring would stop the shivering of his spirit. He said they had roast beef for dinner that night, but the smell was too sacrilegious so he had soup and sandwiches instead.

My friend Jim rang me last night. He said Sister Susie told him he might go home soon, if he sleeps every night. He said he went for a walk around the grounds on his own and noticed the trees were starting to blossom. He said he saw little green shoots straining out of the ground, and the sparrows had laid eggs and wasn't that special. He said he was sorry if he'd saddened me at all, and he'd told Sister Susie she needn't check his room anymore. He said someone had a birthday and they all had some cake, and he went back for seconds, and even for thirds.

Sister Susanne Singleton rang me last night. She said my friend Jim won't be ringing anymore.

The Tracks of Patsy Cline's Tears

Doug Green

AAP: A carpenter from Fractured Heart, the object of an extensive manhunt, has emerged with severe sun-blindness after a month and a half in the desert. He maintains that he was lured there by the voice of Patsy Cline and that he survived by drinking her tears. Doctors are hopeful of a full recovery.

This story in the *Fractured Heart Echo* fuelled much hilarity in the local inn that night. The jocularity centred on whether the song that lured him into the desert to follow a long-dead country singer was 'Crazy' or perhaps 'I Fall to Pieces'. Whether he was sure it was Patsy Cline's tears he was drinking, whether it was really the sun that had sent him blind, and so on. In general, the type of crude banter that characterises the collision of man and alcohol in bawdy-house. As the evening wore on and the rationality wore away, buffeted by a solid wash of cheap hooch, bravado piled upon bravado, dare upon dare, challenge upon challenge, drink upon drink until a torrent of alcohol and bluster swept me over the falls to an inevitable oblivion.

*

She was standing so close to the open door that it took a second for me to focus. Underneath the requisite blonde flounce was the bargirl from the inn the night before. Behind her stood a callow-looking youth and a giant bear of a man with a scarred face.

'Yes ... uh ... How can I help you?' I stuttered, quickly removing the barb from my voice that was reserved for anyone waking me prematurely after a night of revelry, barring a pretty woman of course.

'We're off to see the carpenter. Remember?' she said breezily in a singsong voice, regarding my crumpled, oversize bed-shirt with obvious amusement. An image of Judy Garland as Dorothy flitted across my consciousness.

'I . . . uh . . . oh yeah.' I placed her now. She had spent considerable time the night before, apprising me of every man who had ever done her wrong. I listened but my sympathy had waned noticeably when she firmly declined to add me to the list. She was still nervously fingering the heart-shaped pendant hanging from her gold necklace, a gesture that had so amused me the night before: a whore with a heart of gold.

'Ask what time it is,' she suggested as my gaze settled on her companions.

In a foggy acquiescence I turned to the bear-like man. His facial scarring was so extensive that I could barely manage to look at him.

Dutifully I asked, 'What time is it?'

'It's a quarter to midnight in Boston,' he boomed.

'Ask him what his name is.'

I complied.

'It's a quarter to midnight in Boston,' he boomed again from some dark and deep interior continent.

'Ask him what he's doing here.'

It wasn't necessary. I got the picture. I'm quick like that.

This phrase was his sole conversational gambit, a shield against all the arrows of polite inquisition. Not only did this place his chronological veracity in doubt, but I would say it indicated a significant point of developmental arrest. As I struggled to assimilate him into my poisoned comprehension, I was startled by a loud snort. I spun to the youth from whom it had emanated but there was no rupture in his composure at all.

'He's a mute,' the bargirl offered. 'He just snorts from time to time.'

It was all too much.

As the cold water bit hard into my blotchy skin, the full extent of last night's braggadocio revisited me. Yes, I had suggested speaking to the carpenter this morning. Yes, I had suggested an expedition tracing his tracks. Yes, I had characterised those who weren't willing to accompany us as being full of drunken talk. Yes, I had been full of drunken talk.

*

'It's out there,' he croaked in a plaintive voice, cradling my shamefully soft and pale hands in his large coarse ones. The carpenter raised his bleached eyes to mine, 'What you're lookin' for. It's out there. I've seen it.' While he occasionally muttered or, more disconcertingly, broke into strains from 'Crazy' and 'Life's Railroad to Heaven', he seemed adequately coherent for a supposedly delusional man. Many do.

We arranged to meet him two days hence on the outskirts of town and bade our leave. As we walked away he beckoned me back.

'Mr Snape, Mr Snape,' he rasped in a conspiratorial tone. 'It's all for nothin' without these.' From an old sack he produced a small heart-shaped box and a glove.

'The tears, the tears belong in here,' he entreated.

I opened the delicate lid and gazed into the box's hollow interior.

'And this here glove,' he continued, 'is woven from the finest filaments of wist and lament. It's the only material delicate enough for her tears.'

It seemed like a fine silk to me but, nonetheless, I took the objects, thanked him and bade farewell.

*

The sun rose like a guillotine blade. A motley crowd had gathered on the outskirts of Fractured Heart on the morning of our departure. There was a gaggle of women from the Country Women's Association selling scones and jam while others sat in deckchairs knitting and chatting. The blind carpenter was there. Unfortunately, we were there as well.

My misgivings concerning this outing had increased with my sobriety. I had bragged myself into a corner from which there was no honourable retreat. I reasoned that a couple of days in the desert would provide an interesting adventure (at its best, blonde in nature), a rational excuse for return to town, and many free drinks at the local inn.

The carpenter obligingly pointed in what he claimed was the right direction. Hoping for a convenient out at an early stage, I tested his claims empirically by turning him around and starting him from various points. Each time he swung back to point in the same direction, due south by my compass. It was strange, eerie even, but not debatable.

We began to walk. As I turned around to wave, the carpenter was still standing there pointing, like some crazed Washington on the prow of a boat, surrounded by a gaggle of crones whose demeanour owed more to Goya than benign nature. It occurred to me that there was a whiff of absurdity about this expedition. I, Lesley Arthur Snape, milliner to the nearby town of Eastwood, was leading an expedition comprising a lumbering bear of a man with a scarred face and limited discourse, a mute youth who snorted like a pig and a whore with a heart of gold. We were setting forth, on the say-so of a blind carpenter, to seek the tears of a long-dead country singer in the middle of a desert. I can only entreat you to believe that I am a sane, rational person of superior intelligence (someone much like yourself) and that I came to this enterprise bristling with the fearsome armoury of an arch sceptic.

As a lone black crow floated lazily overhead, we trudged single file into the yawning red interior. Ahead, the undulating dunes dotted with occasional spinifex and driftwood. Behind, Fractured Heart diminishing into distance and memory. At first the whore with a heart of gold chattered away cheerily, bubbling with memories of passion, tryst and adventure, but gradually the monotony of our task and the insistence of the sun, bought her attention. Eventually only the rhythmic snorting of the mute youth provided a percussive accompaniment to the day's trek. Later, as we sat down, weary, a warm breeze brought with it a disembodied whistling sound. We were all startled at first but everyone, except myself, seemed satisfied with my explanation that it was just the wind remembering a tune it had once played through the limbs of trees long gone. On that note we brought a close to the first day.

*

The sun rose like a guillotine blade. There was an air of excitement in the camp. The other three eagerly contemplated the carpenter's prediction that we would encounter the first of Patsy Cline's tears on that day. Even the mute youth was snorting like a hungry piglet at the feed trough. I was excited for different reasons. I anticipated suggesting to my comrades at the end of the day that, our mission having yielded no result and having been revealed as the spawn of drunken lunacy, we should cut our losses and head back. Another leisurely two-day stroll through the furnaces of hell and I would return to dine out forevermore on the tale. Of course I kept my reasoning from the others. They were simple in their beliefs, honest of heart, and I saw no reason to infect them with my cynicism.

As we started walking, the others looked relatively fresh and unscathed. I had noticed on the prior day, with some curiosity, that I was the only one who seemed to sweat. Consequently, my clothes appeared sodden and slept in, as indeed they were, while those of the others appeared no worse than when we left Fractured Heart. My legs were also stiff and sore, unaccustomed as they were to exercise, while the others still appeared to have a spring in their step. I was especially stunned by the whore with a heart of gold who had worn lace-up boots with high heels all of this time. Initially I had tried to dissuade her from this foolhardy act, but she felt it was more important to stay in character. Perhaps she was right.

Two events of note transpired that second day. Firstly, the lone black crow that had followed us from Fractured Heart was joined by another, flying in from the east, then two more, until, finally, we had a large cacophony of crows following overhead. Under normal circumstances this would seem to be a peculiar occurrence, but somehow it melded perfectly with the logic of our situation. In any case, this was shaded into insignificance by the second event.

'Look, look, look!' shouted the whore with a heart of gold. It was late afternoon and, as the whistling wind laced its way through absent limbs, something fluttered in the distance. The mute youth snorted enough for a whole farmyard, the giant bear of a man excitedly told us the time in Boston, and I felt my gut tighten as we approached.

It was a tiny white boilersuit, such as worn by a child, fluttering from a bough stuck into the sand. On the back was embroidered 'Winchester Women's Home, Virginia'. Beside it, half buried in the sand, lay a wooden crib with a couple of slats missing. And beside that, in delirious contrast to the red of the sand, lay two glistening, perfectly formed teardrops.

I felt faint. I felt sick. The whistling of the wind, the cawing of the crows, the snorting of the youth, the pounding of my heart. Awhirl, in a roaring vortex of pulse and sound, I dropped on one knee beside the tears. How could this be? Perhaps the carpenter planted them. Perhaps one of the others had planted them. It made no sense.

A great mitt of a hand clamped my shoulder as I reached down to touch a tear. 'It's a quarter to midnight in Boston,' he earnestly warned.

I viewed him quizzically for a second. 'Ah, the glove. Of course, the glove.'

He smiled, or perhaps it was just a scar.

Donning the glove I scooped the dirt underneath the tears and lifted them. The dust dissipated through my fingers into a crimson mist leaving two shimmering little crystalline thorns succulent with heartache. They rolled effortlessly off the glove into the heart-shaped jewellery box. I watched them traverse the perimeter, come together then separate again, before I carefully closed the lid.

That night I was troubled by the day's events, not least because they removed my rationale for returning home early. I was also unsettled by the hundreds of eyes that glinted in the light of our makeshift fire as the crows settled in for the night around our camp. I slept alongside the whore with a heart of gold but, by this time, home was of more interest to me than her favours. The vast litany of men (she even mentioned names in her sleep) that she claimed had done her wrong gave me pause for thought. Even if the amount of wrong done per man was strictly circumscribed there hardly seemed time in her short life for this amount of perfidy. I didn't fancy joining the Dishonour Roll and, besides, after two days of tromping through an inferno, I had very little wrong left in me. I had come to see her as a rather one-dimensional character.

*

The sun rose like a guillotine blade. I hadn't slept well. Upon awakening, I hesitantly checked the little casket but, sure enough, there they sat: plump, obstinate and glistening, impervious to analysis.

Today we composed a symphony. However, I feel I have to preface the story with an explanation lest you think it's pure fiction. We had been in the desert for three days. All visual landmarks had long since disappeared. It was just undulating red sand dunes in every direction, dotted with the occasional spinifex. This sense of physical dislocation coupled with the blazing, maniacal eye of the sun, constant, unblinking, did unusual things to the human psyche. Space and time, torn from their moorings, accrete to phantoms and gnaw at the human sensibility like malign rats. Perhaps a derangement of sorts. Perhaps a perfectly sensible adaptation to one's environment. Cast the first stone if you dare. I still felt perfectly rational, sharper and clearer than ever, living very much in the now. Only it was a different now.

As we trudged to our destiny, the cawing of the crows and the regular snorting of the mute youth brought ideas of rhythm and composition to mind. These congealed into the following sequence, backed by a constant rhythmic underpinning of the crows' cawing:

The youth snorted.

'What time is it?' I asked.

The youth snorted.

'It's a quarter to midnight in Boston.'

The youth snorted.

We repeated this sequence as we walked and I found I was able to syncopate our call and response around the regular snorting of the mute youth. Sometimes I asked the question earlier, sometimes later. Everyone entered into the spirit and the hours passed in relative harmony.

As afternoon wore on, the din of the crows forced us to increase the volume of the symphony. Eventually we paused and gazed up at them, much as an exasperated conductor might gaze at a recalcitrant rhythm section. They seemed to be squawking and fighting among themselves.

'There it is. Look!' squealed the whore with a heart of gold. We followed her gaze to a rag fluttering in the breeze. As we approached, it became apparent that the rag was a tattered white party dress affixed to a bough in the sand. It was the type a young girl might wear to a birthday party. A 13th birthday party to be precise. It appeared to be stained with dried blood or chocolate. And there in the sand, sparkling, pristine, were two little tears.

As we lay down to sleep that night, warmed by a fire of spinifex and driftwood, I opened the heart-shaped casket and gazed at its jewels. Four precious little beads torn from the soul of a long-dead country songstress. I tilted the box and they trailed around the edges in single file, chased each other, merged and emerged. It gave me an odd satisfaction as I lay my head down clutching the casket to my chest. A hundred gimlet eyes flashed ferociously, like stars, in the firelight as I crossed over.

*

The sun rose like a guillotine blade. We formed our single-file configuration and set off. The crows formed their usual vociferous umbrella, shielding us from the harshest of the sun. It had become increasingly obvious to me that there was an essential element missing from our symphony. We had a baritone, we had a tenor, but we needed a soprano, a leavening touch.

'No, no I won't,' she fulminated. 'I don't come from the South. I would never say that.' I had struck that bane of the composer's life: a temperamental diva. I had no idea why she had such a particular fix on this phrase or what it represented in her life. I didn't wish to delve into her psychology but the composition demanded her participation and my focus was burnished into a laser. She ceded to art.

Snort.

'What time is it?'

Snort.

'It's a quarter to midnight in Boston.'

Snort.

'Well, I do declare.'

Snort.

The extra voice increased the complexity of the symphony markedly. Now there were three separate voices to syncopate around the mute youth's rhythmic snorting and we amused ourselves by stretching the simple structure to its limit. There is something reassuring and slightly hypnotic, even meditative, about such a repetitive formulation and time passed in musical idyll, if such a thing be possible in the furnace of a desert.

Towards late afternoon, as the wind picked up, bringing a woodwind section to our symphony, the crows became loud and argumentative again, squawking and pecking at each other. We followed as this thrashing and darting throng crossed over the peak of the next sand dune and there, amid the cacophony and spot-lit in the shadow of the crows' mass, was something glinting in the red dust: three golden rings, a bunch of scorched flowers, a broken whisky bottle and two quivering tears.

The tears rolled off my glove into the casket where, combining with the others, they nearly covered its bottom. As I observed this growing collection with a sort of pride, a low mournful howl emanated from the east. We all turned to look. Even the crows fell silent. It could be the wind. It could be some poor beast wounded in love. Whatever, we decided to spend the night there.

*

The sun rose like a guillotine blade. No one had slept well the previous night. The crows had been querulous and restless. The unearthly howl had reappeared several times. The mute youth had snored. Nonetheless we wearily formed our single file and began trudging. The crows testily rose aloft to form their umbrella.

There was no question of a symphony today. No one was in the mood and the crows were far too noisy. From the start they appeared agitated, swooping and thrusting their beaks at each other belligerently. Amid this, the whore with a heart of gold turned back to me.

'You know, I've heard it said that the mystery of life is contained in a bird's swoop. In that singular parabola the possible is simultaneously circumscribed and exalted.' She turned back and continued trudging. It was the only thing she said all day. I was amazed.

By late afternoon the aggression and screeching of the crows had reached its crescendo. My head was splitting. We stopped and looked upward at this teeming black swarm continually swooping on its own centre. Suddenly a single black shape was ejected from the middle of this seething mass and sailed over the crest of the dune we were climbing. We clambered our way over the top just in time to see a lone black bird roll on its back and expire. It had run out of space to sculpt and time to steal.

A bed of diamonds sparkled around the black sheen of the fallen aviator. On closer inspection it was actually a rhinestone covered dress of the deepest blue that the bird's landing had uncovered. The dress was badly burnt around the edges and had a yellowed piece of paper pinned to it. It looked to be a boarding pass dated March 5th for a flight from Kansas City to Nashville. And there, beside the dress, two tears.

The tears rolled off the glove into the casket. I didn't need to prompt their movement as I was shaking involuntarily. I looked down. They had congealed into a mirrored surface covering the bottom of the casket. A huge flash went off in my eyes as the sun caught the surface, momentarily blinding me.

Blinking, I looked down again to see a stranger reflected in the mirror. A hard angular face burnt lean by several days in unrelenting sun and several decades in unrelenting life. A face burnt spare of wonder, chiselled free of newborn hope. I felt giddy. I heard a booming voice, 'It's midnight in Boston.'

The tremor that had been building inside suddenly flung me, like a rag doll, to the sand. Then far beyond.

The sun fell like a guillotine blade. I tumbled into a twilit canyon populated by memory. I saw a shivering child standing outside an orphanage in an exotic location. I saw a smashed back door swung open in a genteel suburb. I heard shouting and begging and pleading. I saw a startled dog scurrying for cover. I saw a dark, cruel stranger who wasn't someone else.

And on this vertiginous descent, as I plummeted whistling through a boundless canyon of memories towards a heavy core, I clutched to my chest a small and delicate heart-shaped casket of Patsy Cline's tears.

Hinterland

Susan Errington

When at last he came to the city of his dreams, Dan Nerrida rented a small flat on the outskirts of the metropolis. His apartment, two rooms in all, was on the 11th floor of a grey tower and from the window he had a view, between the buildings, back across the dusty hinterland to the tall city. It backed onto the train lines and, at night, when Nerrida was asleep and everything else was still, the sound of the great transcontinental trains would enter his dreams. In his sleep he would cross deserts and skirt rainforests, he would rush past numberless towns and dawdle in nameless cities. Nightly, he traversed the nation, ocean-to-ocean, hearing, above the train's metallic lullaby, breakers smashing on the reefs or the fierce sea, wind rushing in to carve its breath on the white sand hills.

In the mornings when Nerrida awoke in his own bed, he was exhausted from his travels. He would stumble about, remembering that he must go to work, searching for the clothing he had laid out the evening before. When he was finally showered and dressed, he would sit at his kitchen bench, gripping a cup of instant coffee and stare, bleary eyed and sleepy, down the narrow channel towards the great city as if searching for stars through a telescope.

His work took him away from his city. An old bus carried him further into the industrial zone to the place where he was employed, not as you might think – not as countless immigrants in the past had laboured, as the servants of the serpentine assembly line – Nerrida did not work like that, but in a cramped, dusty office above the factory floor, a box perched on metal stilts, whose only windows looked out over the machinery and the workers. Sometimes, thinking about a problem, he would walk to the window and watch the progress on the line. Often, while Nerrida stared down on this industry, a worker, as if aware of his presence, might stop and look up at him, unsmiling, and after a moment turn away. Nerrida would return the stare without acknowledgement. The tremendous noise of the factory floor lay like an unbridgeable chasm between him and the worker. He always waited until the worker had looked away first, then went back to his computer, to the numberless piles of forms, claims, charts and statements that were his work.

He had few visitors to his airy retreat, except the mail boy with more paperwork and sometimes the floor supervisor would come in at 11 and share a brief morning tea. The supervisor, as a friendly gesture, always brought sticky buns filled with mock cream and thin strawberry jam.

'Much quieter in here, eh mate?' the supervisor shouted, and Nerrida, for whom there appeared little difference between the decibel level inside his glass-and-plywood cell and that outside, would nod and smile. The noise of the factory, Nerrida realised, had gradually worn away the supervisor's hearing.

On such mornings, Nerrida would finish his bun quickly and the supervisor would leave. Then he would turn back to the computer screen that was gradually wearing away his eyesight.

In the evenings, when work for him was finished, the same dilapidated bus carried Nerrida back to his apartment. At this hour, there was also a change of shift and the bus was crowded. Nerrida would stare out of the window, lulled into dreaming by the murmured, weary conversation of the factory workers. During these times, as he counted down the landmarks on his familiar journey, the sewerage works, the abattoir, the dam, tangled thoughts came to him. He reflected how his going home from work brought him closer to the great city of his dreams than leaving his homeland. A kind of reverse journey, he thought, too tired to carry his idea further.

Home. He turned the key in the lock and went in. He put his bag down on a kitchen chair and busied himself in the bathroom, washing his hands and face. He whistled and hummed snatches of tunes and wished that he had a radio or a television to put on as background noise. The sparse stillness, the empty quietness and order of the apartment, always disturbed him. For reasons beyond explanation, it made him feel that he was dead. He went to his briefcase and pulled out the newspaper. He had already examined it at work, but he sat down at the kitchen table, shaking and crackling the stiff broadsheet, and started reading it again. Later, he decided he would put on some toast and open a can of soup. He always took his main meal at lunchtime, in the factory cafeteria, where the bland, hearty, subsidised food proved cheaper than what he could shop for and cook himself.

By the time he had finished with the paper, it was seven o'clock. He looked up, feeling a change in the air as the growing darkness seeped into the apartment. He could see the lights in the buildings in the great city. He folded the paper and went into the bedroom. Every evening at this time, he phoned his wife and daughters. The little girls knew that the call was coming and the telephone would barely ring more than once before the receiver was snatched up. Then Nerrida would be buried in an avalanche of childish words, the day would be breathlessly spun out for him, he would hear the name of every friend, the progress of every lesson, the menu for dinner, who had come and gone to the house, the school. Afterwards, his wife would come on the line and they would talk about visas and money. Sometimes they argued about the visas. His wife worried that he wasn't doing enough to reunite them, and in her voice he heard her fear that she was losing him. He could hear how tired she was, how lonely, and he longed to hold her in his arms and let her rest there.

After talking to his wife, Nerrida felt alone and unhappy. He went back into the apartment's larger room that served as both kitchen and living room and poured a glass of water from the tap. To create the illusion of space, the room had a long bank of windows on one wall and it was through these that Nerrida contemplated the great city. The large windows also made the apartment cold at night. That evening, Nerrida did not want to look out and he closed the grey venetian blinds against the night air.

Nerrida thought again about his wife. She was wrong. He loved her more than ever. He hated asking about the visas, the bureaucratic labyrinth, the endless, exhausting telephone conversations with faceless officials. He was wearied by the slow grinding away of his hopes. Sometimes many days would pass before he could make another call.

Nerrida wandered around his living room, but there were no pictures on the walls or other decorations to distract him. He stopped at the mantelpiece over the gas fire to look at his photographs and books. There were assorted pictures of his wife and daughters. Nerrida studied them briefly but did not pick up any. Next to the photos, a small row of books stood between two fruit tin bookends. He reached out and caressed their spines. He had brought these few favourites with him but most of his books had been left behind. Nerrida owned many books. He remembered the texture of their words, the smell when you opened the pages. He realised that he missed his books as much as he missed his family.

On impulse Nerrida removed a book from the row and flicked through the pages. It was *The Call of the Wild*. He had loved this book as a boy. This copy was very old; the pages were worn and faintly discoloured. The book had been given to Nerrida's father as a school prize. Nerrida turned to the front and read the inscription, set out in perfect English copperplate: 'Awarded at the Penang Free School, Dux of English', it read, and then the year. George Town, Penang, George Town, Jamaica, ports of a dead empire. His father had been a ship's captain.

Nerrida decided to take his father's book to bed. He read until midnight but afterwards found that he could not sleep. His mind churned with the words of the book, with family conversations, other, disparate voices. At last, just before dawn, Nerrida fell into a light slumber. He dreamt that he was with his dead father at the factory. In the dream his father told him that he was about to be deported.

The next morning was Saturday and Nerrida did not have to go to work. He lay in bed, watching the sunlight make patterns on the wall of his bedroom. Through the slats in the blinds, he could see strips of the deep-blue sky. He got up and decided to do his washing. The apartment building had a single communal laundry on the ground floor, reached from the outside.

When he came down into the lobby there was a small blonde girl sitting on the front steps by the common entrance door; it was not possible to get past her. He put down his washing basket.

'Excuse me,' he said cheerfully.

The girl, whose back was towards him, turned her head but did not move. She stared coolly at him.

'Excuse me,' he said again, wondering whether he could step over her. The girl was very small. To his relief, she stood up and let him pass. At the laundry, his arms full of the washing basket, Nerrida turned to push the door open with his shoulder. The little girl was standing behind him. Her wide blue eyes were fixed on his face. Nerrida jumped in surprise. He put his basket down again.

'Hello,' he said. 'Do you want something?'

He did not want the girl to follow him into the laundry where they would be alone.

The girl did not answer but went on staring at him.

'Are you looking for someone? Your mum and dad?' Nerrida was beginning to feel uncomfortable. As far as he knew there were no children living in his tower block, no families. The residents were mostly like him, working men living on their own.

'Do you understand?' he asked the girl, and suddenly a thought came to him. 'Do you speak English?'

But the girl remained silent, seeming to understand but not speaking. He looked around, desperate to see another person. At the side of the building, near the laundry, was a long, bituminised strip of land, used by some of the tenants as a car park. Nerrida hoped someone might come out. To his immense joy, he saw Sylvie walking towards him. Sylvie was one of the few women living in the tower.

'Who's your friend?' she asked.

'I don't know. She's just wandering around here,' Nerrida explained. 'Listen Sylvie, can you help me? I think she needs to find her parents.'

'Brett's coming to pick me up in a minute.' Brett was Sylvie's boyfriend.

'She can't stay with me.'

Sylvie sighed and looked at her watch. 'Let's go up to your place and call the police.'

*

They waited for the police in Nerrida's flat. Sylvie stationed herself by the window to watch for Brett. Nerrida watched the girl as she circled his apartment, her intense gaze taking in the details. She stopped at the mantelpiece and pointed to his photographs.

'Do you want to see them?' he asked her and, this time, the girl nodded.

Nerrida picked up a picture of his wife and daughters, and knelt down beside the girl so that they could both see the smiling faces.

'This is my family,' he said, telling her the names of his daughters.

Nerrida stared into the depths of the photograph. It was one of many that he had brought from home. He had looked at this picture many times, but as he spoke to the girl about his family, Nerrida realised that he could no longer remember when and where the picture was taken or even if he had been the photographer. He could speak only of the impersonal features of the photo. It appeared to be a warm day, his daughters were wearing light summer dresses, and their hair was tied back in long, neat plaits. Behind them was a green blur of either ferns or palms, he could no longer remember which. Was it a special occasion? Nerrida wondered. He was afraid. It occurred to him that his memory of his family was becoming this photograph, a small moment in time, tightly framed and without context. The girl moved closer to him and he could feel her warm breath reverberating in her little body. Nerrida and the girl stared at the picture together and, though there was no resemblance, he felt suddenly that she could have been one of his daughters. He would like to turn his head, he imagined, and see her there beside him, transformed into his own likeness.

Nerrida put the photograph back on the shelf. The girl pointed again. The other object on the mantelpiece was a large crucifix of polished ebony, standing on a thick base of the same wood. It bore a silver figure of the crucified Christ, a little tarnished with lack of cleaning. It had belonged to Nerrida's grandmother. Nerrida did not carry the crucifix with him for devotional purposes. The crucifix was a piece of his home, his history, his greater family. Nerrida reached up and took the crucifix down for the girl to look at. She stroked it gently.

'Shall I tell you a story about my grandmother?'

Again, the girl nodded.

Nerrida remembered his grandmother best on the verandah of the house in George Town. There she would tell him stories and it was there, when she was very old, that she had given him the crucifix. He was 11 at the time and immensely proud to be chosen to receive this artefact. His grandmother, his mother's mother she was, had been born in Jamaica. Her ancestors had been brought as slaves from Ireland to work the English lands. She would tell Nerrida stories of these days, so she claimed, and her young grandson loved to hear them, sitting on her lap or at her feet.

The girl smiled as Nerrida talked and he felt encouraged.

'Her name was Mary Kathleen O'Connor,' he said, speaking of his grandmother. 'Her island skin was the colour of smooth, milky chocolate but her eyes were the pale, fragile blue of the northern summer skies on which they had never looked. Blue like yours,' Nerrida said to the girl and she smiled again, a little more widely.

'Brett's here.' Sylvie's voice broke their dreaming. She rushed to the door. Nerrida followed, taking the girl by the hand.

'We'll wait downstairs for the police,' he said to Sylvie's back but she did not answer.

*

Nerrida and the girl waited on the footpath, choking a little in the fumes of Brett's vanishing car. It was very quiet. The sun was hot on their faces. In the distance a whistle blew and the girl turned in surprise. Behind the building, she could see the sleek images of trains as they flashed by. The girl moved closer to the train lines.

'Don't go too far,' said Nerrida, afraid of losing her now. 'The police will be here soon.'

The girl came back to where Nerrida was standing. She reached into her pocket and pulled out a scrappy, torn piece of paper, holding it up for him to read. It was a page from a domestic train timetable. As Nerrida studied it, another train whistled, pulling into the station near the grey tower block. Nerrida looked up, distracted, and the girl ran. She ran down behind the building to the track, her pale hair flashing in the sunlight. Nerrida followed, wrong-footed by surprise. He called after her but she did not turn. He followed her onto the platform and through the doors of the train. The train's doors closed with a hiss. The girl went to a seat and positioned herself by the window. Nerrida sat down beside her.

'Where are we going?' he asked, but she gave no reply.

The train carried them into the great city, to a large station, and Nerrida knew where they were. He occasionally made this journey himself on a Saturday or Sunday. He would get off at this very station and wander aimlessly in the streets for a few hours, only to return home feeling desolate, his dreams disappointed. For a long time, he'd wondered why he felt this way.

Nerrida looked down at the girl. She knew where she was now and she was leaning against the window, pleased, excited even, to be somewhere familiar. She looked up at Nerrida and smiled. He smiled back.

'Nearly home,' he said to her and the girl nodded.

It was because he was alone, Dan Nerrida realised. That was why he was disappointed by the great city of his dreams. It was a dream to be shared.

When the train stopped, the girl jumped up immediately and led him out of the door, across the station, down flights of stairs, through archways and corridors until the maze brought them to another platform and another train. This was the train, he remembered, from the girl's timetable. The girl ran on and took another window seat.

Dan Nerrida did not follow. He stood and looked at her through the glass and she back at him. As the train began to move, the girl raised her hand and waved to him, slowly at first and then faster in a frantic gesture of thanks and farewell. Dan Nerrida waved back, and went on waving until the train had disappeared, carrying the girl home.

Dan Nerrida stood for a moment on the cold, subterranean platform, staring down the dark tunnel towards the tiny arc of bright light at its end. Then he walked back towards his own train. Reaching into his pocket for coins, Dan Nerrida pulled out the girl's tattered timetable. He turned the paper slowly in his hand, and as he did, he thought about the visas for his family. He would make another call in the morning.

Walking the Thin Edge

Katherine Doube

We are, officially at least, nowhere. We have been stamped out of Thailand and are standing on the muddy banks of the Mekong wondering whether to negotiate our boat across in baht or kip. If we are officially nowhere, are we freer than ever or are we more trapped? Can we float away into non-existence or do we have to smile at the bureaucrats and hope they don't find a reason not to stamp our passports?

A man perched on the rim of one of the boats looks at us expectantly.

'Sawadee karp,' Michael greets him. 'How much to take us across?'

'Thirty baht.'

'Each?' Michael asks, pointing first to himself and then to me. 'Thirty, thirty?'

The man nods. Michael looks at me. I nod and the man indicates for us to pass him our packs.

On the other side of the Mekong, we climb out and, after getting stamped back into existence, enquire about boats to Luang Prabang.

*

Our first night in Laos is spent on a small, lumpy double bed, the heat lying like a film across our bodies. The fan's sweeping move-ment echoes in the mozzie net.

'Do you miss your girlfriend?' I ask Michael across the space between our pillows.

'Of course.' He rolls onto his back and stares up at the netting above us. 'But she's not here and sometimes I forget.'

'You think she's here too?'

'No,' he laughed. 'No matter how much she claims she hates London, Katie would never come here. "Too many bugs, too much dirt!"' he exclaims in imitation. 'No, I'm just kind of, here, you know?' He turns his head to face me. 'And that's all there is for that moment.'

I roll onto my back and run my eyes over the net above me as I try to think back to moments of *now*.

'Sometimes,' he says, 'travelling, it can make you so removed from yourself that you are more yourself than ever.'

Wandering the world without people who have already boxed you, I think, and spot a tear in the net.

'Look,' I point up to it in the top left corner. 'I'm going to have to sew it.'

'Just leave it, Jess.' I'm on the wall-side of the bed so any getting out to get something will naturally be done by him.

'The bastards always find a way in,' I joke, 'and I'm the one with less vitamin B in my blood, so I'll be the one in itchy agony tomorrow.'

He groans.

'And I'm not taking malaria tablets, so imagine how bad you'll feel when you desert me in Luang Prabang to catch your plane, if I'm alone *and* sick.'

'Fine.' He pulls the net out from under the mattress and swings his legs down. 'Where is it then?'

'In my top pocket.'

He rummages through my pack. 'This?' He holds up the small tin in which I keep my sewing kit.

'Yep. Thanks, Michael.'

He climbs back under the net. 'You should be used to "mozzies",' he says, as I stand up on the uneven mattress, 'you're from Australia.'

'But I'm not from Queensland, and I swear these tropical ones are different.'

'Yeah, yeah.'

I reach up awkwardly to sew up the hole in the corner.

'There's another.' Michael helpfully points to the net near his feet. I finish the one I'm on and start to sew that one.

'There's one,' he says.

'Stop looking,' I scold, joking. 'The more you look, the more you find. It'll be never ending.'

'I just want to protect you from the blood sucking vampires,' he protests innocently.

'Ha ha.' I sit back down on the bed. 'Okay. Is that the worst of them?'

*

We sit for two days on hard narrow wooden seats and watch the banks covered by trees slide past as our boat chugs down the Mekong. We see an elephant lifting logs on the edge. Occasionally we pass a village and wave to the children who play in the water.

Evening on the second day and someone in front of us points to a town where two rivers converge. It is hidden by the steep banks, trees and concrete walls that protect it from the Mekong in flood.

We climb stiffly out of the boat and up the concrete ramp for our first glimpse of Luang Prabang. We follow the road along the river until we see a sign for a guesthouse. We get a twin share and dump our bags.

Back on the street we look both ways. Compared to Thailand the street is empty. Up one end we can see people setting up small stalls on the ground and lanterns lighting up like fairy lights.

'That way?' I suggest and we start walking.

We get to the top and turn to walk between the rows of rugs with lanterns, T-shirts and Sa-paper displayed on them. Behind the goods, people eagerly watch us approach. Mostly the stall holders are busy setting up and chatting among themselves and only watch us out of the corners of their eyes, but some call out, 'Lady, lady, you want to buy scarf?'

We reach a smaller alleyway and turn down it. There is food stall after food stall, and we both suddenly realise how hungry we are. We wander down, looking at the sausages, the pastries, the Mekong seaweed, chicken meat held between split bamboo over roasting flames. I buy some fresh spring rolls, after watching the woman roll them, and although I only pay for four the woman puts in a fifth, smiling and nodding at me. Michael buys a plate full of food and we sit at the table next to the stall.

'I love this place, Jess.'

I nod, my mouth full of fresh rice paper and mint.

'The people are so chilled. I wish I could stay longer.'

'Then do,' I say, impractically.

'I can't. I want to spend a couple of days in Vientiane, and my plane leaves in a week.'

'Back to the job and Kate.' I stick out my bottom lip and pat him on the arm. 'Poor Michael.'

'But it is like that. I don't want to leave. I don't want to go back to that me. I want to travel forever!'

I laugh. 'Me too. If only, right?' When I get back I have to start applying for jobs, enter the 'real' world, armed only with my blunt BA.

'It's all right for you,' he says, 'you've still got a month left.'

The time is already uncomfortably close, and I push it from my mind.

'Just think, you're going to see Kate, that's worth it, isn't it?'

'Yeah,' he concedes. 'It'll be good to see her again.'

We wander back through the narrow streets to our guesthouse where we fall into separate beds.

We look at each other across the air space between us.

'I'm glad we met, Jess,' Michael says. 'I'm going to miss you.'

'You're not going for another two days,' I protest.

'But still . . .' We lie quietly for a while.

'It's a pity, you know,' he says, 'that I'll never travel with Kate. It's something special.'

'Mmmm.' Sleep is drifting towards me.

'Are you rocking?'

'Mmmm?'

'From the boat?'

'Night,' I mumble.

'Fine then,' he says, in a mock huff. 'Goodnight, Jess. Happy dreams,' he says, quoting what the fresh-spring-roll lady had said to us when we passed her again on our way home.

'Happy dreams,' I say, and sleep safely enclosed in my mozzie net.

*

The next day we wander through the quiet streets of Luang Prabang. The whole town is heritage-listed and each French-style shop and house, each wat, is beautiful in itself.

We find ourselves sitting on a wall on the side of a road watching people ride and walk past. On the other side of the road is a wat and in the courtyard some young monks, dressed in their bright saffron. The noises that float over to us sound like play, and I'm shocked to see one of them smoking. I point it out to Michael.

He laughs. 'In Thailand, they're members of gangs. Didn't you see the tats?'

I look at him, incredulous. 'Are you serious?'

'Yeah,' he insists, 'some of them.'

We fall silent again as a tuk-tuk drives past. The monks come over the fence and talk to some children who are passing.

'Have you ever had a moment of pure happiness, Jess?' Michael suddenly asks.

I laugh.

'Right now,' he pats my knee and looks away from me, down the street, 'is one.'

'I've had one of those.' I nudge him with my body. 'Coming down from a trip, for half a second everything just made sense.'

He laughs. 'Can't you take me seriously?'

I look up and down the street. To our left some women sit in the doorway of a house, chatting and sorting chillies, to our right the road slopes away, lined beautifully on both sides with buildings and effusive plants. Across from us we can see a saffron robe drying in the window of the building next to the wat. A burst of laughter floats over to us from the monks.

Again I lean into Michael, our bodies making light contact before I sway back straight.

'You're right,' I say. 'It's beautiful.'

Revisit

Emilie Field

Hung out between two worlds to dry, I fall
into the folds of time and miles and self.
'Your passport please' – yes, yes, I qualify –
my name is on your faceless list. 'Proceed
to baggage claim,' retrieve the dying em-
bers of remembered life. 'The customs line
begins just there.' The ashen morning paints
dark yellow shadows on my face. Too tired
to bear the grating 'Welcome home!' Oh, let
tomorrow forge its curse in stone! Today
smells oddly of the past: I want to sit
alone a while until it's out of reach
(no place was ever faithful). 'Now, you must
be glad to be at home again' as if
my life had been on hold. If only I could
drop the cup politely poised for talk
of trifling things and watch it shatter. Don't
you see, your rapture is my exile.

Reasons for Green

Chelsea Avard

Reasons for green today: *accord, aesthetics, aetiology, affiliation, affinity, Australia, birth, bafflement, beatification, celebration, Cork, culture and custom, death, dice-rolling, ease, effect, effort, emigration, fairytale, faith, family, freckles and freedom, the whole gamut, genuflection, genus, graveyard, hardship, homesickness, Ireland, iridology, irresponsibility, inebriation, jealousy and justice, keening, kinship, kiwi and kookaburra, liver and lifeline, Mother, mental health, mass consciousness, naivety, Nana, numerology, obligation, occasion, that it is not orange, paradigm, patriarchy, poverty, queeredness, rebellion, resonance, rootlessness, sentimentality, substitution, synthesis, tales, theatre, top of the morning to you, undercurrent, Utopian dreams, veins, vestiges, vibrations and vision, wagers, welfare, whimsy, whorls, the missing letter in a generational equation, yearning, zeal, and zodiac, and zygote.*

Today I wear green for you Derry. Green skirt, green shirt, green shoes, even an emerald hidden in my navel. A visible, public action with private reasons. A New Zealand born Australian woman singing to bring harmony to her relationship with the Irish grandfather she never met. Searching Derry, I'm still searching for ways to combine our souls. I must begin somewhere, so I paint myself grass, to imagine my becoming. Shallow and external, yes. But perhaps it is best, in our case, to keep tangible activity gentle and non-transformative, and leave hard metamorphosis metaphorical. Never having seen you, touched you, smelt you, heard you, I have lived my life with only a taste of relation, the blood I might lick from a pierced fingertip. So, yes, perhaps this is why green is important. Heartstrings may survive spiritual teasing as I pull green weave over my skin; veins are too fragile for tugging. You might never have worn green. You might think my efforts ugly. Sprung of one green country and jumping to another, you left progeny with feet itchy enough to keep moving. I am left with a deep-seated need to mix green and brown. My jade belt secures for me my birthplace as well as yours.

The history of Saint Patrick's Day is well documented. Little of your own story exists on paper, County Cork one of only a handful of verifiable facts. Your children met you rarely (one not at all) and suffered under your successor in the household, an Englishman with hate enough for an entire nation. My mother and her siblings hold you only within their minds. Father-love, and fear, desire and fantasy and myth create and obscure you, and of course, the world intrudes, and history colours. You were Derry. You are father, grandfather, saint and scoundrel, drunkard and gambler, seller of children's beds for debts, storyteller, grandmother's sweetheart, derelict, debaucher, silver-tongued, green-eyed, red-haired, loved and loathed, loving and leaving. Also known as Derek McCarthy, Rod Carey, Patrick Leary, Patrick McCarthy, Patrick Roderick Carey, husband of many, protector of none. Wanted for traitorous acts, wanted for terrorist loyalty. Wanted, wanted, wanted for abandonment, theft, indebtedness, gun-running, wanted for 'sins which cannot be specified in this publication', wanted for Daddy-duties, wanted for knee-capping, wanted by six hungry, lonely, sad and forgiving, or desperate children, who wanted to believe you were a prince.

My mother, her brothers and sisters ached with this desire even into adulthood, living despite it (all but one). Suicide and alcoholism stand out, like brown sun-stains on white skin. Their futures echo your past. Bi-polar. Borderline. Post-traumatic Stress Disorder. The modern labels being used to describe the legacy of your failure.

It is a new freedom they fight for. All but one fled the grassy hilly country of their green past and flew to new lives in a browner country, kept kiwi in the sad New Zealand night-time of their hearts. All but one laughed sarcastically with the kookaburra at life revealed by the piercing, white, unsoftened light of Sydney.

Parentless, Peg, Denise, Patrick, Derek and Michael warded off homesickness in a land that flamed red and exploded, leaving the clouds of their homeland to cry for you. Only Nick stayed behind. Looking for you under every sodden leaf and finding only worms of doubt, he fell, following you, down into the brown bottle. He finished things quickly. A simple step onto the black asphalt, timed to connect his tired self with the speeding blue lorry, and he was gone.

It was on the trip home the children took to bury their brother that they found their father at last, pinned down finally in one spot, beneath the same Christchurch cemetery earth as Nick, ten plots down. A shocking symmetry. A small, greying stone with his original name carved deep. 'Dad,' my mother whispered, nudging Peg. 'Shit,' Peg prayed, plucking at Denise's sleeve. 'Roderick McCarthy,' Denise shouted to Patrick. 'Sly Old Dog,' he grinned, waving Derek over to the group. 'Holy Mother of God,' cried Derek in an approximate Irish accent, dragging an angry Michael by the collar. Michael stood and scowled at the sagging grave that told them the last 20 years of Nick's search had been spent chasing a ghost. He spat tobacco-tinted fluid towards the find: 'Fucker'.

Cirrhosis, they discovered in the local records. A rotten though unsurprising end. Putrid brown of family organs now fertilising dead land. Sad, but at least final. Release for you from a scolding world, and for your children an end to exhausting hope.

As for me, you never hurt me to make me spit. Or cry the way my mother does. I have never needed you physically. But today I wear green. I wear green because my horoscope this morning read: 'Wear green today. Avoid excessive alcohol consumption. Contact a relative who loves you. You will find something a long time lost. A green stone will bring health to the internal organs.' I wear green today the way I wore my mother's stilettos when I was five. I wear a green skirt and feel it circle when I turn. I think of Nana at 16 and how you must have made her laugh. I wear green shoes and do not kick my girlfriend's shins as she leans over my desk to kiss me in the middle of the office. 'Happy Birthday,' she jokes, and we flash white teeth at my blanching co-workers. I play with the green stone at my centre during lunch and wonder what you would make of Nina, but not for long. You never were much for society anyway: my picture of you conforms only to stereotypes. I do not have to, and cannot, call you grandfather, only Derry. Derry the green ghost. I am without you and I do not know you well, and yet, as an ancestor, I know you are with me and within me. I blame you, and snicker with you secretly, when I win and when I lose.

I thank you for taking the gambling gene with you to the end. I thank you when my hair glows in the sunlight. I thank you for the stories. I thank you for my poker face. I thank you for my mother. I thank you for my mother. For eyes that match my shirt. That I cry easily. I thank you that I cry if someone dies, if someone lives, if the news is bad, or good, if I hurt, if I laugh, if I am tired, if the song arcs, if the painting reaches my heart, if the book speaks, if the sky is blue, if the clouds are white, if the bush is brown, if the hills are green.

I curse you when my skin burns scarlet in the sun. I curse you when my eyesight fails. I curse you when I drink and drink and drink. I curse you when I smoke all day and cough all night. I curse you when, distracted by thoughts of far-off hills I have never seen, I forget to water my own lawn. I curse you when I forget I am not single. I curse you when my deepest desire to disappear stands facing my desire for Nina. I curse you when my appreciation of the moment leaves me with a depreciated bank balance. I curse you when my only mail is red. I curse you that I cry easily. If the bush is brown, if the hills are green.

Reasons for green today. There are only three: you, and me, and everything in between.

The Dog

Blake Jessop

the dog is bloated and pregnant
and wheezing and happy
bunched up like garbage bags

there's a joke here
I think
in the words basset hound
as I stare at my instrument
imagining meanings
imagining sound

Sounding Silence

Lesley Williams

We should ... say how we inhabit our vital space, in accord with all the dialectics of life, how we take root, day after day, in a corner of the world.

—Bachelard, *Poetics of Space*

This is where I live. A town identified by a mountain that overlooks its valley of broad grassy hills, defining creeks and large gum trees. This is *country,* whose ancestors are, that once belonged to, the *Peramangk* people. The valley has since seen two incarnations. First, it was re/formed by farming. Now it is being re/cast as a mosaic of business, industry, and houses.

All through the town, trees are disappearing one by one, each a sacrifice to the deafening stealth of technology, each one chain-sawed, log-chipped, leaf-mulched, stump-munched. Trees that showed their tops above the town yesterday are gone almost without trace today. Owls, rarely heard, exchange long hoots across the dawning valley.

Houses vanish. Machinery roars through nights filled with artificial light. Streets are reassigned to supermarkets, department stores, variety stores, and car parks. New surfaces, new facades. The building that once was the Governor's Summer Residence is refurbished, restored, and attached to a cinema complex and tavern. Further out, new houses are plastered across old flood-plains and up against hillsides.

*

Once upon a time, for the people living here, cupped hands in a running stream or a welling spring may have been all that was needed to drink. The creeks that run through this valley cannot be ignored. This is high rainfall country; when it rains, the creeks run, water insists upon its presence.

So the paths of the creeks are forced underground, under buildings, into pipes. The rushes and trickles of water, echoing an eclipse of the self the creeks have become, are silenced, just at this point, at this time, in this place.

In the middle of town, where the work is unfinished, one section of creek, running between ruined houses, remains un-piped, open, flowing when it rains, awaiting its fate, collecting: so far, draped along and trapped between its banks, it has a selection of supermarket trolleys, food wrappers, plastic bags, old shoes, lumps of concrete, shards of glass and sheets of tin, and the round dead bole of a tree. Across this wasteland, a profound silence that no one seems to notice, drowned in the drone of de/construction.

*

Can you de/construct a tree?

The last trees to go were three big old plane trees that edged one of the main roads of the town. These trees were on the roadside. The road has been widened. The trees took up the footpath.

What it brings, their loss, is a space aghast with silence, a space that is spare with silence, a silence that is loud in its execution. Not knowing where to go, it sits on the side of the road. Not knowing how to fill itself, it hovers where once leaves flourished.

Three trees: girths much greater in span than a large human hug, munched. A round scar on the ground the only sign of their ever being: they have become mulch, sawdust. Quickly, the path is re/covered with red concrete pavers. A strip of open ground is left along the roadside. More trees will be planted, they say. Old roots will wither and die.

*

All the while, beneath the grid of streets, crossing the creeks, effluent pipes tumble their own dark rhythms and tunes.

All these con/tributaries flow down toward the lowest stretches of the valley, to where Mt Barker Creek, once known as *Laratinga*, runs south-east, out to the plain, out to the Bremer River, out to Lake Alexandrina, out to the dredges pumping sand at the River Murray mouth, dry banked against the Southern Ocean, about 55 kilometres, as the crow flies, almost due south.

The effluent from the town runs into ponds that have, up to now, been emptied into the creek. Now, a wetland has been constructed to take the effluent overflow, to filter, to re/cycle, to provide water for irrigation, and a habitat for birds and other creatures.

*

Here are the wetlands, land based, at what was once the edge of town, constructed as if they were an aquifer, located between earth and sky, perched above Mt Barker Creek. The wetlands are named Laratinga, woven of earth, water, reeds and trees, a place for pollutants to subside, and for birds, insects and frogs to reside. Wildlife and humans alike seek its life, its seasons, its sounds, its silence.

Silence?

Not in the constant hum and roar of traffic on the roads that intersect at the edges of the wetlands. Not in the high pitched sound of a chainsaw.

Not in the alarmed whirs and clacking quacks of ducks as they are disturbed by walkers, who pass by the reeds at the margins of the ponds, where other water-birds chit and chirp and chatter.

Not in the rush of water into the ponds, fed mechanically by pumps, out of the effluent ponds a pathway's walk away.

The day is still. Perhaps silence hides in the leaves of eucalypt that hang in bunches and swags, in acacia and melaleuca, hard-leaved or prickly, in reeds growing tall out of boggy shallow stretches of land that almost allow the ponds to be joined. Old, old red gums along the creek raise bent, shading limbs, and dwell in the silence of time. Swallows flit and soar across sun-soaked surfaces. When swallows fly, the flick of their wings has no sound. As if there is a visual dimension to sound, their flight speaks the impulse of space.

Perhaps silence has weight and movement, like water, and some sinks, some hovers at the surface, some moves with the wind, some moves with the earth, some moves through spaces created by the shapes of apparently solid things.

*

In the background, the mountain.

There is a map. Dated 1944. Printed on paper welded to cloth. Showing the hills, the contours that form the valley of the mountain. Showing the streams that run down from the hills, into the deepest valley, into the largest creek, out through the hills to the east. In 1944, the valley was filled with farms. There was an ice cream factory, a tannery, a railway station, and roads criss-crossing the valley, out to the farms, all named, on the map. This was dairy country, and the place where a subterranean form of clover was discovered, developed, and grown as pasture, lapping up the high winter rainfall and the hot summers, replacing the dry grasses that were here when settlers first arrived. And the Governor's Summer Residence had become a Rest Home. And the creeks ran through the back yards of the town. 'The Mount', marked as tight contour lines, shaded brown, reaches to 1680 feet.

*

From the plain to the east, the mountain is a beacon. It is a mountain defined by relationship to the surrounding country, rather than great height. The summit was the place where, in the past, people smoked the bodies of their dead. Through the back of the mountain runs a fault-line, exposed in the quarry on its northern edge. Climb to the summit and the ridge of rock that faces the setting sun denotes its lifted edge. If the fault is its hinge, the ridge is the edge of its doorway.

The mountain was *Womma Mu Kurta*, 'the hill above the plain', to the people who came to it from the east. Its name was *Yaktanga*, or so the legend goes, to the Peramangk people who lived along the waterways, beside the springs, across the grasslands and beneath the trees of the valley. Its name is Mt Barker now, in the wake of Collett Barker, 1831, explorer.

Drive up to the mountain. Give yourself distance, space, silence.

Perhaps.

There might be a car filled with young men, radio blaring, pot smoke writhing, beneath the bristling red mast of the radio-telephone tower. There might be a family racing to the top, voices shrill to carry them up the path.

Climb to the summit. Sheoaks pick up the wind in dark, needled branches and toss it down the slope with a noise like the sea. Yellow-wings sip at banksia flowers. Correa and hop bushes, leaves parched as summer closes and autumn begins, line the path with dry twiggy stems. Cars on the freeway below buzz and hum. A butterfly captures sun on a rock. Small fine-leaved xanthorrhea, stems squat and twisted beneath the tuft of their leaves, hundreds of years old, are dotted across the sloping back of the rise.

Sit on the upturned parapet of stone at the rim of the mountain. Think about time. Sit on this warm squared weathered rock, look out across the open well of the valley and see it as time. See time as desire, memory, loss, e/motion. See time as a well.

A well is dug into the earth and lined with stones. Beyond its wall, earth presses, trickles through gaps, silts up the water. The well fills, and moves, and holds. Water floods, seeps, trickles, drips, splashes in, flowing down hillsides as streams, rivulets, through soil, between rocks, filling aquifers, soaking the ground. From the well water is hauled, or seeps away. All the events of its lifetime are held as rings, ripples, splashes, watermarks, and the sound of itself, being and always becoming.

All events, all stories, flow into time, are absorbed: each event, each story, existing in its own past/time, in/visible, silent, filled with un/reality, absorbed into itself.

Imagine yourself, intrinsic to time.

*

If time is a well, at the end of a life, the well would be full, not necessarily to the brim, allowing for events of filling and emptying.

Its water could be used, even wasted sometimes, but the events and the nature of its coming and going would be the time of its life.

*

I have this idea of the silence of sound, an image of sound, a feeling of sound, silence 'speaking volumes'[1], silence as a carrier for listen/know/ing, silence as a perturbation toward some 'understanding of what it is that you meet'[2], the paths you will follow, how time will fill, where you are placing your feet.

Endnotes

1. Paul Carter, 'Speaking Volumes' in *Poetics in Architecture*. Guest editor Leon von Schaik. London: Wiley Academy, 2002: 11–13.
2. Watson, Irene. Conference Keynote Speaker, *In Conversation*. Adelaide University, 2001.

Scissors, Paper, Stone

Dena Pezet

Small, larger, even larger, larger still, then largest. The drops of blood thread across the kitchen floor, each growing exponentially like a string of cheap beads, only disappearing when we darken all of the lights in the house. The doors are locked and barred shut with chairs, but from the window we can see the burning tip of his cigarette glowing in the dark across the garden.

Ray uses his hands, his fists, and so my mother usually doesn't bleed, but bruises flowery and purple like exotic violets. Ray expands when he drinks, becomes twice the man he actually is. His conversation becomes more fluent, confident, discursive and easy. Inebriated, Ray understands his place in the world, however temporary and drink-fuelled it might be. And it's usually a good place, a better place. A place where he is full of sharp ideas he can articulate eloquently, secure in the broad sweep of his own knowledge. Ray throws money around when he drinks, nothing is too much trouble for him; he is a good guy. He's benevolent, munificent, respected. His self-image peppered with adjectives that would have no place in his unoiled, abstemious world. In drink, he often recalls his time at college, how interested he was in philosophy, literature, the arts; how far he could have gone had circumstances not moved against him. When Ray drinks he maintains that drinking is good for him, all the way up to and way past when it isn't.

*

Ray slides his eyes across the living-room floor, over the length of me, consuming my legs, my chest, my face; his gaze thick and greedy.

'She's probably too old to be sharing a bedroom with him,' he says, his eyes never moving from me while his head jerks towards Gabe. Ma tilts her head to the side and drags her eyes from the TV quiz show, pondering this revelation, but she loses the moment.

'Can you give me a famous philosopher beginning with K, please?' Bob, the TV quiz show presenter, asks.

'A famous philosopher beginning with K, Ray?' Ma says in response to Bob. 'Who would that be?'

'Beginning with K?' Ray murmurs. 'Hmmm, let me think.'

'Keynes?' Gabe suggests.

'Keynes was an economist, you idiot! Bob wants a philosopher, a philosopher. Jesus,' Ray says. 'It's Kant. Must be Kant. Must be.'

Bob tells Ray that he's correct and that he's on his way to a 'Gold Run'. Ma gives Ray a round of applause, one hand empty, one hand wrapped around a glass of brandy, the liquor spilling all over her wrists in distinct amber cords.

'Did you know it was Kant, Franca?' Ray asks.

'Yes.'

'Really? How come?'

'We're doing Kant and *The Critique of Pure Reason* at school,' I say.

'I loved philosophy when I was at university,' Ray says, pouring himself another drink. Ma and Bob interrupt his reverie.

'What was the full name of Kant's major work on morals?' Bob asks.

'What was it, Ray? What was it, Ray?' Ma bubbles.

'I know this, I know this,' Ray says excitedly.

'*The Groundwork of the Metaphysics of Morals*,' I say. Ray stiffens, frowns at me, the air around him almost congealing.

'Smart arse,' Ma says to me as Ray stretches across her to switch off the TV. It seems that I have misunderstood the rules of this particular game. Behind Ray's back Gabe rolls his eyes at me. I shake my head as slightly as I can at him, mouthing 'No', then we just sit quietly watching them both drink. Not speaking, just waiting.

After a few quiet words with Ma, Ray finally switches the TV back on and we listen to Bob, who is still doing his stuff.

'She shouldn't be sleeping with him, it's not right at her age,' Ray eventually starts up again, bringing his fist down on the arm of the sofa with a whack. He looks at Gabe, who immediately looks away.

'Can you give me a famous battle between the French and English beginning with W, please?' Bob asks.

'What do you two do in there all the time anyway?' Ray says, ignoring Bob for the moment.

'We just talk,' Gabe says, turning his head to look at him, eyes wide at the stupidity of this question, the obviousness of the answer. We do talk, we talk a lot as we snuggle side by side, like two orphans together in my dead grandmother's old double bed. It still faintly holds the persistent tang of Gabe's bed-wetting. We can both smell it, but neither of us ever mentions it. Gabe sleeps badly, he has a history of unruly evenings, bed-wetting, nightmares, crying out in his sleep. Sometimes he gets up and sleepwalks around the house. There have been times when I've found him outside in the bitter night. The snow falling or the rain teeming down, Gabe usually just staring into the dark or out to sea, calling quietly but repetitively for my father, nothing on his feet but the cold.

'Waterloo!' a contestant shouts at Bob in glee. We don't know if he's correct because Bob has to go and the show's signature tune starts up.

'You talk?' Ray says to Gabe, inflecting the second word in disbelief. 'And what do you talk about?' He's watching me, his stare setting me in aspic. He rapidly jabs his tongue at his top lip, the way flies test food before eating and then regurgitate their own filth.

'Just things,' Gabe says casually. Gabe doesn't know where this is going, but I am onto it straight away.

'Gabe has nightmares. He walks in his sleep. Someone has to stop him getting up and falling down the stairs. Last time he dislocated his right shoulder,' I say directly to Ray.

'I bet that put his right hand out of action for a bit,' Ray sneers. My cheeks burn and I can't look at any of them, and I imagine that if Gabe understands, he'll be the same.

Bob is telling us to watch tomorrow when we'll be getting the answer to that last question.

'Oh Ray, stop being silly,' Ma says, playfully slapping Ray in the chest. He kisses her on her nose and tickles her under her ribs, his hand edging higher and higher 'til it cups her breast. He looks at me and squeezes it hard. She giggles and snorts and drops the glass of brandy she is holding. It soaks her skirt, the stain bleeding further and further across her lap, but she doesn't notice.

'She's old enough to be in her own room, on her own,' Ray perseveres, his tongue still doing the fly thing.

'Leave them, Ray,' Ma finally cuts in. 'We don't want him falling down the stairs. Anyway, come on. We're going out. I've had enough of this.'

He staggers up. 'Yeah, come on. This is boring me.'

*

Although he leaves the bar before her and it takes her some time to pull herself together and have that last drink on the house, she gets home before Ray. Even as she crashes through the door I can almost feel the house tensing as the walls brace themselves, jittery in anticipation. I suppose any house holding my mother would always be a random, unstable house with a volatile temperament and every day in that house would be disjointed. But the events of this night seem especially fractured. With Ma things rarely unfurl sequentially, unfolding smoothly across seconds, minutes and hours, but this night seems particularly frenzied and incoherent to me. It takes no time and, at the same time, takes forever.

She tries to tell me what happened in the bar, but can hardly speak, her tongue fat and slow with alcohol and her mouth hamstrung by the rosy swelling of her face. I don't get much out of her at first . . . hand . . . smack . . . fall. But it turns out to be a long night and slowly I piece it all together. Was this the first time he raised his hands to my mother? She'd have you believe it. Every time.

'Love, like hope, has four letters,' Ray had apparently said to her through the smoky hub, earlier that night as they drank in the

Oyster Bar. She must've been nearly as drunk as him as she nudged her bar stool away from him.

'Yeah?' her creased, over-made-up face said.

'Yeah,' he said, taking another swig of his drink. 'Two vowels and two consonants.'

She laughed. Drunk, stupid. With her attention wandering, she stood up and signalled to the waiter, 'Hey!' then pointed at herself, 'More champagne for the lady!'

Ray grabbed her arm. Slowly he tightened his hand around her thin wrist, carefully increasing the pressure. Then he squeezed hard, pulled her back to the seat and hissed, 'But you know, the vowel alone has no audible friction. The consonant needs the vowel to form a syllable, to create resonance.' His spittle bubbled at the corner of his mouth and she snorted out loud, collapsed into laughter.

'What are you on?' she squealed.

'But don't you see Ruthie?' Riled, urgent now, he said, 'We need the cooperation of both to form words, to construct language.' He took out a pen, started drawing diagrams on the bar in lurid green ink, scribbled furiously, attracting a heavy stare from a bouncer. 'There's got to be a lesson there.'

'You think?' she sneered. 'Oh just shut up, Ray. Just shut the fuck up. Let it go, we all know you went to college. Big fucking deal.' She knocked back the dregs of her cocktail. 'But hang on!' she flashed, 'I forgot! Didn't you get kicked out of school?'

'I had to leave. My father couldn't afford the fees,' he said stone cold.

Then she cackled recklessly, the gin having really got hold of her.

'Fees my arse! You were kicked out. Kicked out for being a dumb fuck. He couldn't pay. Wouldn't pay, Ray, wouldn't pay because he knew you were a dumb fuck and that's all you still are.' Ray just kept on with his drinking, right through this, the hidden voltage building but not yet ready to ignite. She went on, 'Franca's right. You are a dumb fuck.'

'Franca said that? No, she wouldn't say that,' he said, shaking his head, a grin ambling across his face, dozy and slow. 'Franca understands me. She's a bright kid, that girl.'

'Franca, Franca, Franca. Oh fuck Franca! Get with it, Ray, she plays you along. She thinks you're a dumb fuck who doesn't know jack shit about anything.' She wiped her lips with the back of her hand, smearing her lipstick around the line of her mouth and down across her chin. 'And she's dead right. You are a dumb fuck, a boring dumb fuck and a fucking boring fuck!' She disintegrated into laughter, delighted by her ingenious word play, everything around her loud and frantic. In the desperate push of the Friday-night grab at cheer, nobody noticed this lush at the bar, this man with her, primed and ready to snap.

As the harsh glare of the bar lit up her once beautiful face, Ray apparently slapped her hard with the back of his hand, his signet ring gouging out a piece of her cheek, just above the bone. The blow caught her firmly. She reeled backwards off her bar stool and landed solidly on the bar-room floor. She sat with legs awry, her skirt riding up past her stocking tops. She slumped forward, silent and vacant, like a broken doll. In one second, hand, smack, fall: the elegantly neat equation of violence. Ray drank up carefully, left a tip for the barman and left.

Was this the first time he raised his hands to my mother? She'd have you believe it. Every time, so she could freely give him 'one last chance' unburdened by any contradiction of conscience. My mother doesn't understand the principle of contradiction. Even if she did, she wouldn't believe that a proposition and its negation couldn't both be true. When Ray says he hits her because he loves her, well, she believes him. To her the latter doesn't necessarily deny the former. All her life she's been waiting for some man to bring a fairytale her way and for most of the time she thinks this is it. Does my mother have an absolute view of the world? Without a doubt, she absolutely does. Is it uncontaminated by any kind of rational objective experience? It most certainly is. My mother is an empiricist. She believes that you have to live life to know it. That true knowledge comes through experience alone. Ergo, my mother's experience and thus her knowledge, which can never be separated from her own raddled, drunken world, are warped and perverse, but to her it's real. And in a way, by implication, it is real for me too. It is how I live.

*

As soon as Ray is through the front door she's at him. She grabs at his eyes with her nails, digging them into the soft and vulnerable meat of his sockets, cursing and screaming like a banshee. It is late, he doesn't expect it and is unsteady on his feet. He falls over onto the table, with her on top of him, falls heavy and loud, bringing what was there crashing to the ground: tea, sugar, cups, saucers, a loaf and, discrete as an afterthought, the lonely chime of a bread knife hitting the flagstones.

When he gets up he looks huge and angry, like a rhino penned on some hostile grassland, heavy, furious, snorting and powerful. He charges at her, his hands at her throat, and slams her up against the kitchen wall, her head banging back against the brickwork as she goes. It all happens so quickly and yet it all happens so slowly. I make no noise. I am totally numbed, can neither move nor speak, and I feel nothing, just look on. Somehow her hand finds a bottle of milk and she brings it up in a firm arc across the side of his head.

You need to know that milk bottles and beer bottles don't smash in the same way. Take one in your hand, feel how rigid and smooth the glass is against your palm, wrap your fingers tightly around its brittle neck, hold it squarely and try it. Look closely, milk bottles tend to shatter, splintering out into tiny rubbled shards, leaving your hand empty, bereft, while beer bottles tend to crack and split along crucial angular lines, from base to girth, leaving something in your grip, something that can be used again later. It's to do with the quality of the glass used for each – the basic price people are prepared to pay for nourishment, and the higher, more inflated price they will pay for booze.

The blow to his head, heavy and dull, sounds like a big exploding egg being dropped hard on the floor. He doesn't fall again, just gently bows his head, blood trickling down his face from a wreath of a dozen wounds that ring his forehead. He is already slow and dazed from the drink but none of this makes him stop and he goes at her again and again and again and this time he is bellowing, raging loud and hard, and just over this bellowing I hear her screaming and I hear myself screaming and then she's screaming again and it all runs into one cacophonous mess and I still don't feel anything but before we know it, suddenly from nowhere, there is blood everywhere, more blood, blood on Ray's shirt, blood all over my mother's new dress, all over his shoes, blood on the floor in which he stands and slips. Small, larger, even larger, larger still, then largest. The drops of blood thread across the kitchen floor, each growing exponentially like a string of cheap beads. And she is screaming at him again and again and again and then, without a word, he just backs away.

The power sputters out of him. He holds his hand up to his face in disbelief, his expression stock-still; he just looks at himself and wipes his own blood on his already sodden shirt. Confused, he staggers, wonders where it is all pouring from, wonders what the fuck has happened.

'Get out! Get out, get out!' she just keeps screaming at him and I close my eyes and I feel him shove past me and I hear the back door open and I hear him stumble out into the garden and when I open my eyes again he is gone. She locks the door, piles chairs at the handle and we darken all the lights in the house, but from the window we can see the burning tip of his cigarette glowing in the dark across the garden.

We race around the house, frantically checking windows, the front door, and almost trip over Gabe sitting, as unmoving and as hushed as stone, on the stairs in the dark. Later we sit huddled on the kitchen floor, the three of us with our arms around each other; just like a family. I don't know how long we sit there, maybe hours. Perhaps at different times of the night, Ma or Gabe sleep. Occasionally maybe one of them moves and the other also moves to accommodate, to regroup and find the optimum position. At one point she kisses me on the forehead, takes my free hand and tells me it will all be all right. And you know, at that moment, my arm around her, the three of us clutched there together on the chilly flagstones in the dark, I don't feel cold and I don't even mind the warm stench of the alcohol on her breath and despite myself I believe her.

I do not sleep that night and at some point Ma huddles Gabe off to bed with her, but I remain alone downstairs in the dark. I don't know where Ray is. The chairs are still stacked at the door handle, the back door still locked. I pick through the debris of the night, remove the chairs, open the door and go out into the garden at the side of the house.

It is one of those rare, mild and pale nights that you sometimes get in the very north of England at the peak of summer. Nights when even the dark sky seems luminous and occasionally you can see a faint trace of aurora borealis, colouring up the heavens.

The garden is vast, walled on four sides by misshapen stone blocks, slathered with concrete and crept with trailing, unnamed vines. I stand back and stare at the house, black against the sky. I know every brick of it as well as I know my own face. That house, the desolate roll of the salt marsh at its rear, somehow always deferring to its natural backdrop and somehow always waiting. I feel I am always waiting with it. Forever a sense of being watched, I am always, always watchful.

The moon is so full and so bright you would swear it could burn and I see Ray clearly. He is slumped in a heap on the ground, out cold, but probably not from his injuries, probably from the drink. He lies there bloated and stinking in his own piss, grunting and snoring like a bull seal baking in the sun. The wound is partially hidden by the fold of his stomach but seems to have stopped bleeding. Although it looks deeper than I had imagined, it is only a flesh wound, flabby, serrated and pulpy. I stand there for a while just studying him. Gradually I realise that I am still gripping the bread knife, which has never left my hand all night. I notice that I am breathless, that I am panting like a dog, elated, edgy, so hot-wired that I could blaze across the sky. Ray's blood is all over my hands, is all over my skin, set dry and rough, that skin on fire with my new discovery. I nudge him gently with my foot. Not too hard, it's almost a gesture of solidarity. He doesn't stir and I sit down next to him and for the first time in hours I put down the knife, laying it out in the moonlight, the blade bright, stark. Looking at the sky I understand. In that moment I understand it all. It is vivid and clear. We are the same now, Ray and me. No longer just antagonists, polar opposites, but now bound together, partisan, proponents of our own code; violence and power our common parlance.

Self-Portrait at 26

Emmett Stinson

A misanthrope, perhaps. One who rarely
Gives more than he gets. Surly when he drinks.
Deemed inconsiderate by those he's barely
Met, because of shyness. Sometimes he thinks
He'd be better off a bit less bookish.
An odd fish. One who prizes rarity.

Sometimes his opinions are too intense;
What seems dire one day will soon be replaced
By an opposite conviction, or sense
That what he'd felt before was effaced
By contradiction. He's often selfish,
A cold fish, without love or charity.

There are justifications he has made
For his casual negativity,
But they're anodyne. A sham. He's afraid
Of dying, mourns his own mortality,
Hides truth behind a shade, forges a wish
For absolution, feigns sincerity.

The Parents

Rachel Hennessy

Peter Kay had forgotten where he put his pipe. It happened often now, about the same number of times he forgot he smoked a pipe at all, reaching for the softpack of cigarettes he had smoked in his younger days.

He shuffled into the kitchen, sure he'd find the pipe on the side of the sink, stuffed bowl spilling drops of tobacco into the chrome grooves. Enough to drive Irene crazy. He slid one slipper after another to make less noise, gliding over the linoleum like an Olympian skater in his final. What would he score? Not much, and not a pipe. The sink siding was empty. Always losing precious things.

'Shit,' he said and turned his head a little, just to make sure Irene wasn't there. He knew she was lying on their cream bedspread with the window open, enough to catch air without making a breeze. It was 6:30 am and he wouldn't see her until eight when she'd emerge, fuzzy-faced, to fill a thin glass with water from the tap, take a sip that would turn into a gulp and start scrambling eggs for breakfast. Still, Peter turned his head when he swore. The pleasure of speaking the word 'shit' wasn't outweighed by how much trouble he'd be in if Irene heard him.

Where was that bloody pipe? Sliding on the lounge-room carpet, he saw immediately that it wasn't on his armchair, the next obvious place. Irene's knitting basket sat where it always did, a ball of pale pink wool dangled over the top, stabbed by two needles. Christ, pipe and knitting. What old people we've become! His smile wasn't entirely amusement. He wanted to stride majestically around his house, proudly stretching muscles in pursuit of his pipe, but he didn't just shuffle because of the noise. The movement lessened the constant throb in the joints of his swollen toes.

On good days, they laughed about no longer having specific reasons for physical pain. The simple disease of being old explained a multitude of aches. On bad days, well, he didn't want to think about the bad days.

Out in the garden he was fairly sure he wouldn't find the stupid pipe, but the rising sun of November was soft enough to stand in, to make him forget. Irene's attempt at a water garden, a huge wooden barrel with drowning lily pads, had a peculiar smell and, as always, she'd over-fertilised the azaleas and under-watered the bougainvillea, the flowers of one drooping as a sad puppy, the other fried brown like dog's poo. Peter didn't care much. He liked the fact that Irene's foibles were here, botanically illustrated, even if innocent plants had to suffer. He stood on the cement path that led down to the Hills Hoist. What kind of day would it be?

*

Irene rolled over, trying to get the pillow right beneath her head. It was too thin, this pillow, but Peter's was too fat. When had her pillow become too thin? How heavy her thoughts must have been over the last seven years, so heavy her pillow couldn't cope and had sunk under the weight.

She was being stupid, of course. She hadn't had this pillow for seven years. They'd gone and bought new ones from Target, when? Was it really two years ago now? Last time she'd washed the cases Peter made a comment about the brown stains on the stripped pillows, suggesting that they must've been secretly smoking, as the patches were the colour of nicotine. She hadn't laughed at the time. The jibe seemed like a criticism of her housekeeping. It must've been a bad day.

She rolled over again, the wind coming through the window touching the side of her face. Not a breeze, just the visit of new air. She'd like to sleep longer, but today it didn't seem likely. The minute she thought about time, she felt her body tensing up. If only she could stop such thoughts arriving. She could hear them, creeping up towards her. Before she knew it, they were there in full view, a flood of synapses making connections, taking her back.

Almost seven years.

At least in November she had a little break. There was the approaching nightmare of Christmas, but there were still many months before any real anniversaries. Christmas was almost an escape. The noise and the fuss, drowning in tinsel and tack. Angela, the other daughter, would come home carrying a miniature real tree and their steady friends would drop in, ploughing them with puddings they'd still be eating in March. She had to stop herself this year. She was getting fat.

Lifting herself from the bed, she knew it was early for her to be on the move, but she could surprise Peter.

Through the kitchen window she could see his back. He was standing as if expecting a space ship, his head turned up to the sky, an outline drawn against the light.

Irene lifted the lid of the kettle and filled it with water. She felt sorry for anyone who didn't drink tea, in the way that she felt sorrow for those without children. Immediately she knew she shouldn't have gone down *that* path.

Her forehead began to contract but she didn't want to disturb Peter. Let him enjoy the gentle morning, sky transforming from deep ocean to pale shallows in a slow, magical hour. She would be all right.

Turning, she knocked one of the dinner plates off the dish rack. It smashed. One half stayed together, the other side split into three triangular pieces.

*

Peter heard the dish smash. Irene shouldn't be up yet and early-morning breakage wasn't a good sign.

'You all right, Irene?' he called.

'Fine, love.'

She didn't sound fine but Peter was enjoying the opening of the day, his mind seeping into the quiet beginnings of light, caws of birds settling into the distance where they didn't demand anything of him.

'Irene?'

'Yes, love?'

'Have you seen my pipe?'

'No, love. Sorry.'

He wished he'd found it. He wanted the smooth flow of nicotine in his blood. Angela shook her head at him though he was sure she secretly puffed away herself. She badgered him to stop smoking, but seven years ago when he was on the verge of quitting, they'd lost Cathy, and that seemed like enough to give up.

That was the kind of day it was going to be. The birds didn't help.

The evening remained hazy to him. He'd tried to remember it many times. What TV had he watched? What did they eat? It'd never come back and, after a while, it was too trivial to ask Irene. The police told them the timetable of Cathy's murder, and eventually they'd consoled each other with the fact that they'd been in bed, unaware and somehow innocent.

But he remembered the night. He'd got up to get a glass of water. He'd forgotten to place it on his bedside table before going to sleep, as he usually did. The house ticked with quiet so the water seemed to thunder through the pipes in the walls. He saw Cathy's bedroom door was slightly open and knew she wasn't home. Cathy always kept her door shut when she was sleeping. He took a sip from the glass and reasoned she would have stayed at one of her friends' places. She wasn't a little girl anymore, shouting for joy at Christmas presents. In the hallway mirror, alive with moonlight, he made a face at himself and padded back to his bed.

Their bedroom door had to stay open. Irene was claustrophobic, and the one night he'd accidentally closed it, he'd woken to find her clawing the air beside him, eyes fixed in a glazed state of terror. The image made him forget Cathy's absence, and he'd lain himself gently beside Irene, listened to her sweet breathing.

Lying there that night, he'd been thankful. God had seeped out of their lives gradually, replaced by the noise of children and a mortgage and a six-day working week. But he liked to hold on to some belief even if it wasn't centred in one all-knowing being. Whatever had made it all happen for them, that night he was grateful.

He never told Irene about his trip to the kitchen sink and his dismissal of Cathy. Every year made it harder. How had they become defined by that one night? He felt the surge of anger he had in those days just after when the pack of reporters flooded around him on the courthouse steps.

An albino cat jumped over the fence and landed in the wood-chip mulch of the side garden. No, it had hazel eyes so it wasn't really albino, but its fur was snow white. He hadn't seen it before; most of the local cats were tortoise-shell and scrawny. It stood and looked straight at him. Was he friend or enemy, it asked? With all the anger in his blood, Peter didn't know himself.

*

Irene looked at the broken plate.

On *that* night she had felt Peter climb out of bed. She always woke a little when he made big moves. She knew he'd forgotten his glass of water and felt a bit of guilt that she hadn't checked for him. Was that expected? Even after all these years she was just playing at being a wife, muddling through, worried that the real wives would catch her out.

She heard the water roaring in the pipes and pictured Peter standing tall at the sink, his beautiful profile. A thrill ran through her still that he was coming back to her bed, would lie down beside her, put his hand on her hipbone.

Peter came back into their room. The soft thud of the glass hitting the bedside table and his fumblings to find the edge of the bedspread. He lay on his back and didn't touch her, afraid to wake her. She knew how to keep her breathing even, practised in sub-terfuge from nights of a drunk father stumbling in, his bitter breath washing over her face, 'You awake sweetie?' and having to listen to confusing rants about losing streaks and the next winning post if she couldn't fake descent into sleep. The steadiness of her chest fooled Peter as it had her dad, but there were no bourbon sobs from her husband, his breath getting heavier and heavier, the two of them joining the same rhythm.

When she had been sure Peter was asleep, Irene got up to look at the clouds. It was something she did sometimes. She couldn't say what made her get up some nights and not others.

She padded past Cathy's room. The dark slit of open door told her Cathy wasn't home. Where would she be? Probably at that new friend's house. She'd seen her through the fly-screen door, honking for Cathy in a short red car, a dimpled arm hanging out the window trailing a cigarette. Her voice was coarse, 'C'mon get your arse into gear!' and Cathy had laughed nervously, her eyes sliding to Irene. 'Have a good day,' Irene had said, disapproval staining her words.

That night the clouds were all over the sky, grey with pockets of deep blue. Big fields of moisture wrapping up a couple of stars.

*

Peter reached up and sent the Hills Hoist spinning. With the amount of vitriol running wildly in his body he could imagine his clothes breaking apart as if he was some expanding superhero. The cat saw it, hissed at him and shot over the lawn to the other side of the garden. It could've gone right over the fence into young Melanie's place. No danger there of human activity. Melanie was never up before 10:30am and, even then, she was as ratty as hell if Peter happened to catch her chucking out a bowl of regurgitated meat for Puss-Puss, her tabby. She always looked at Peter as if he was some aging pervert, holding his garden hose, while he forced himself to smile. Could tell her some fucking home truths.

He'd wanted to smash the reporters' faces in. There was one, with round, gold-rimmed glasses pushed back on a nose that looked like a beak. His face had come so close to Peter's, almost touching his damp cheeks. Maybe he'd been pushed in front by the throng or maybe he was a bird, sticking his nose in, sympathy somewhere deep in those black eyes. In memory, that one reporter had animal dimensions. Peter couldn't separate the pupil from the rest. One single orb trying to get into Peter's mind or his heart.

'What do you want to see happen to the men who did this to your daughter?' It was a shriek of a voice, making its way over their jostling heads. The beak-nosed man seemed to repeat the question like a refrain, and it rippled through all of them so there was silence.

The not-quite-albino cat didn't retreat to Melanie's world. It was standing pensive against the wooden pales, tail on antenna alert. Peter wished he had the hose in his hand already. Spray it with a power-jet, send it scurrying away wet.

His father had disposed of an unwanted litter of kittens once by putting them all in a bag and smashing them against a brick wall. The hessian bag turned to red as Peter watched. He'd thrown up for three days in a row afterwards, and his mum wanted to take him to hospital. His father insisted it was attention seeking and that no son of his needed a drip to keep him alive.

'Go on then,' Peter challenged the cat, as if it was the mother of those devastated kittens. As if it had the power to change the timbre of the day ahead, block off the rush of recrimination.

'What do you want, cat?' he almost spat at it.

*

Irene reached down to pick up one of the triangular pieces of ceramic.

She gripped the edge of the sink, noticing how badly etched her hands were, catching the smell of last night's onion in the plug-hole. Or was it in her fingers? Everything stank. No matter how judiciously she scrubbed, there was the stench of the past, the memory of meal after meal. She could dry-retch at the aftermath of rubber gloves and the penetration of cleaning chemicals. She tried to relax her breathing, as the therapist had said, or one of the counsellors. There was a multitude of advice, but only snippets remained with her. It was likely she had mixed them all up into a mass of ineptitude. She was probably doing the one thing she wasn't supposed to.

She had one of the plate pieces in her hand. God, she hated this plate. A spasm of laughter hit her as she thought about how diligently she'd tried to keep her dinner set intact in the early days. It had hardly ever been used, deemed too good for common occasions, kept in some God-forsaken cupboard and paraded in front of Peter's new, to-be-impressed workmates. They giggled at night over the 'Royal Doulton Brigade', but she was secretly desperate for company in their weatherboard house at the end of Holiday Street. They'd been deserted by that lot a long time ago; workplace friendships melted when Peter retired early. None of them understood. None of them knew how often they sank into darkness.

'Stay positive' came into her head in a young, almost sickening voice. She couldn't even tell if it was from a brochure whose tone she'd imagined, or a real person looking at her over a field of brown desk. As if she could plug herself in, hook up to the recharger and transform from negative to positive at the push of a button. The bars on Angela's mobile phone streamed up and down, up and down, sucking up the juice of life just to keep on going another day. As if it was that bloody easy.

Staring down at the floor, at her own long, quivering self, blood had stopped circulating in her toes, the half-top lamb's wool slippers were making her more, not less, aware of the cold. Should have got those ug boots when Peter offered but they seemed so un-ladylike, not part of the wife charade.

What was it that Cathy wanted? Irene was weak with the sorrow of her absence. And yet she was afraid, as if there was something she should have done, some confession she should have made which would give Cathy peace.

The weight of it forced her down onto her knees. To the un-watching world, she was kneeling to collect the fragments of the broken plate but close to the ground she had to close her eyes. The swirl and swirl of Cathy's cry, the colour of the bruises, splashed blood on the wire, thick male laughter. Irene whirred with imagined sights and sounds; her forehead stretched tight against her brain. Vomit crowded into the top of her throat. All was buzz, dots of light. She lost Cathy in the distance, pulled far off into a corridor of black. She couldn't even lift her hand out to try to catch her; she wasn't sure where her hands were, or where her legs started and stopped. Was she sitting or standing? What were her limits? At once she was a field of skin with the power of touching, spreading out, and then she was a tiny thing, hollow and chipped away to nothing.

*

He'd left Irene too long.

'Peter?' her voice cut into him, sounding weak, not at the right level somehow. He turned to shuffle quickly up the path, just registering the blur of white as the cat finally retreated.

Irene was on her knees in the remains of a powdered plate. She'd managed to cut herself, though whether the blood came from her palm or a scratch on the leg he couldn't tell. He looked down at his Irene, her face penetrating the floor, skin pulled tight across her head by reddened hands. Short, shock white hair clipped closely to the back of her neck. He might have died with the pain of it. But he hadn't. They hadn't got him yet.

'Love . . .'

'I'm sorry,' she muttered but didn't move.

*

She couldn't get up. Peter was there, hovering on the edge, but she couldn't find him either. Again, the vomit surfaced and she put her hand up to find the sink. Met by an arm, she touched velvet and her throat constricted into dryness, the hot rush of sick going back down into her stomach.

'It'll be all right, love,' came to her through the buzz, and she caught a moment of Peter, bending down in his deep-blue dressing gown.

She felt herself lifted, not-so-gently yanked by the armpits and deposited. Where was she now? Cathy was laughing nervously, pulling open the passenger door, waving with the other hand. Was it the right or the left hand? Irene was standing on the cement verandah looking stern. The friend butted out her spent cigarette on the car door and let it drop into the gutter. Did Cathy call out 'See ya, Mum!' or was it just the sad chug of an exhausted engine, willing itself into action? The same car that had left Cathy at the railway station and appeared in the line at the funeral. Engine after engine switching off after parking up, edging the bitumen roads that criss-crossed the cemetery. A shout of cockatoos in the sporadic trees, hungry, horrible birds – she hated them for making more noise than she could at her own daughter's burial. In her head, she'd called for someone to shut them up, shut those bloody birds up!

'I know, love, I know,' Peter said.

Irene didn't remember speaking to him but it was all such a spin she couldn't be sure. The darkness cleared and there she was, in Peter's armchair, her cotton nightdress ruined with spots of blood. He was running a damp face-washer along her heated arms. Darting her eyes down, she saw her right hand held a wad of tissues, the bottom layer stained from pressing against the cut in her palm's mount. She couldn't feel anything.

*

'It'll be all right, love,' Peter murmured again without conviction. He knew Irene had gone back to her last sight of Cathy. Or maybe, like him, back to that night when they lay in bed, so sure they deserved happiness, unable to conceive the growth of random abduction and relentless violence spreading like cancer up to their front door. They'd done nothing to deserve it, he thought, but maybe they'd done nothing to not deserve it.

'I'm so sorry, Peter,' Irene whispered down to the ball of tissue. She was actually turning pink with embarrassment, and still he hadn't figured out what to do, how to bridge the gap between them.

He got up from his nursing position on the arm of the chair. The face-washer needed wringing. On his way to the kitchen he knocked the oak sideboard, and his pipe, lying like a wounded soldier on a scarred battlefield, rattled to attention. There it was. Peter couldn't see how he had missed it with such pathetic camouflage.

Picking the pipe up, he continued on into the kitchen, unfound bits of plate crunching into the soles of his uggies. He ran water into the spongy fibres of the washer, letting the sweat run out of it.

The bitterness of onion came out of the plughole. Water sounded through the walls again.

It was almost eight already. The yellow-breasted honeyeaters were hopping into the garden, keen to nip at their fuchsias. The birds weren't afraid of the residue of cat, and they certainly weren't afraid of Peter's occasional rants, swinging with the plastic rake to send them off.

'Aaaaah!' he'd yell at them like an old loon, and Irene would come out laughing, 'You nutter.'

He'd never tell her about his trip to the sink that night. He'd never be able to unburden himself like that, to see sweet forgiveness in Irene's fading eyes. Why didn't he make a phone call? No mobiles in those days but enough landlines to check that Cathy was safe. If he'd worried more, been less self-satisfied, less content, not so keen to get back to Irene's side. Loved her less.

*

Her arms were cooled now. The lounge room had settled back into itself. Her legs were against the itchy tapestry covering of Peter's armchair. It still felt as if all the blood was running close to the surface of her skin, but at least it was in motion. Grief had caught her again, trapped the steady flow of time and held her motionless, put her back in the places she didn't want to be. She tried to fight. She tried to not make comparisons when she spoke to Angela. She tried to watch the plate fall and think it was just the clumsy hands of a decaying woman. But it got her always.

*

He sat again on the arm of the chair, leaning down to put the fresh washer on Irene's forehead. She lifted her uncut hand to hold it there.

Peter couldn't remember how he'd answered the reporter's question. He just remembered the stupid face he'd made in the mirror that night.

'Do you want a cuppa?' he asked, unwilling to let the silence last too long.

'Love one,' Irene answered eagerly; she savoured tea more when he made it.

He pushed himself up again, the winch of his toes telling him he was overdoing it.

*

Irene watched Peter sway slightly as he moved down the familiar track, lost to her across the worn carpet. He stopped just past the doorframe.

'Irene?'

'Yes, love?'

'I found my pipe.'

'That's good, love.'

He disappeared into the kitchen. The day was only beginning.

Inconvenience

Christy Di Frances

Just so inconvenient, this life,
This entire life – life of dirt,
Grubby wet-smudged marks on the laundry room floor.
Oh, that grass-stained laundry!
So much laundry for five small bodies and one primordial man –
Kind, true, but without understanding
Any real sympathy of how truly inconvenient
His seed must have been to
You.
Your life, a mother's life:
Why not complain, Mother, of so much inconvenience?
So much hindrance to all your most effervescent poetry passions
And wanderlust, too.
No complaints, still? As always, even in memory of nights,
Long, sickly nights, winter-chilled nights of flu,
Days spent constantly tripping
Over painted-block castles on the living-room floor.
What? You hardly noticed? Strange.
And you so astute, so thrifty at the shops.
Talented, too – unparalleled among storytellers,
Except for (perhaps) Scheherazade.
But so inconvenienced, Mother, by – well, let's admit it –
Me.
And also my two tomboy sisters,
One brother, strong-willed, mischievous,
A baby girl – fond of her princess-like costumes
All trimmed by you with the spare bedroom lace.
What a queen you were to us then!

But now I see, being taught the embarrassing price of your crown
And you a martyr, really,
Of the swing-filled parks, the apple-pie oven, the story-book nights,
Nights when you could have been out on the town.
So sorry. But at least take regrets from me, your daughter,
And also via me from my corporate-close contacts,
We who are finally free now as birds in our – well, let's admit it –
Cubicles.
We in our power-short skirts all agree,
We of the world without stories excuse you.
But how can we ever find pardon ourselves,
For your being so kindly
Content?

The Family Trip

Rudi Soman

They pulled into the parking bay of the National Park and with a final rev of the engine, Kamir killed the ignition. Why does he always rev the motor at the end? thought Omar. They slowly clambered out of the car. Yasri and Kamir stretched their legs and trudged around the vehicle in an attempt to regain lost circulation. Sam twisted his torso from side to side and juggled his head around on his neck like a boxer limbering up. Omar touched his toes. Kamir began unloading the boot. They each picked up a few items. Kamir looked around for the best way to go.

'Here's a sign,' said Sam. '"To Deep Creek, McKenzie Falls and Bullock Nature Reserve". Ha, ha, you wouldn't want to get lost up Deep Creek without a paddle, would ya bro?'

Omar laughed, but Yasri and Kamir gave them a strange look.

'Okay, we go that way. We find some nice place to eat our lunch near this deep creek. That sounds like a nice thing to do. C'mon boys. Omar, lock your door. Yasri, walk with me,' said Kamir.

The family moved slowly up the path. It was a warm, clear day, and the park was well patronised, mainly by families with young kids and a few scattered couples lolling romantically on the grass. Now and then they would pass a lone male walking on the windy path or sitting on a bench. When Sam spotted such a person he would nudge Omar in the ribs and say, 'Check it out bro, rock spider eh?' and laugh out loud. Especially if the unfortunate man was carrying a camera. 'Why else would they come here? Mate, fucken suss if you ask me,' reasoned Sam to his brother.

They reached Deep Creek and set up their picnic in a pleasant grassy spot under some dappled shade. Omar spread out the chequered woollen blanket. Kamir opened the esky and began to lay out the food. The family sat and snacked on the lunch they had brought, even Yasri, who allowed herself to lie on her side and regally pick at red table grapes like the wife of some Roman senator. Still there was a feeling that she could not completely abandon herself to her senses as she inspected each grape for a deformity or blemish before popping it into her mouth. Omar and Sam munched on *kibbi* and talked among themselves, sitting cross-legged and hunched over. Kamir sat cross-legged too, slightly stiff but relaxed all the same, eating quietly and reading his two-week-old copy of the *Middle East Herald*. Intermittently he would utter a grunt of displeasure at some annoying news. Every now and again he would utter a wry chuckle, possibly amused by the futility of it all.

In this way the family passed an hour and a half, conversing lightly from time to time but without the strained, combative tone of the discussions that had taken place in the sealed environment of the car. Eventually Sam stood up.

'C'mon bro, let's go for a walk. My bum's getting sore from sitting all the time, y'know? Let's go for a walk and stretch our legs eh?' He motioned to Omar with a jerk of his chin.

Omar got up and he and Sam walked up the sealed path that ran parallel to the banks of the creek. As they ambled away, Yasri called out to them not to be too long, as they would be heading back to Greenacres in just over an hour.

When they were out of earshot, Sam said, 'So, bro, you get some *skunk* or what?' and pulled a small metal pipe from his sock.

'Yeah, it looks like it, eh? Looks like a good deal,' Omar said fishing the sachet out of his pocket and handing it to Sam.

'Your cunt mate's deals are getting better, I gotta say,' said Sam, inspecting the firm, pungent buds, the bag cupped in his hands. 'It's like I always say, "Keep the customers happy and they'll keep you happy", you know what I mean?'

Omar had heard this – just one of Sam's business maxims – several times. He had been surprised it hadn't come out earlier during the 'franchise' discussion in the car. Sam broke off the end of a bud and packed the cone of the small metal pipe. Again using a cupped hand, he offered the pipe to Omar as they walked.

'Here you go, bro, you start it up.' Sam always let Omar start the pipe. It wasn't necessarily out of generosity; he knew Omar would only take one deep toke at first, and hand it back, burning just right for the strongest lung-full, a real whack from the cone.

They veered off the path, away from the creek, and headed towards a small thicket of youngish gum trees. The terrain had only a slight uphill gradient. Sam led the way, crunching through the dried vegetation and fallen leaf debris. Omar followed close behind, watching his steps carefully so as not to scuff his new Nikes. After a month they still looked like he'd bought them yesterday. About 100 metres away, they stopped at a place that was well out of sight of the path. Sam handed Omar his lighter, took a cigarette from a packet and placed it behind his ear.

'Okay, bro, let's fire this thing up eh.'

Omar put the pipe to his mouth and lit the cone. The cold brassy taste of the implement soon gave way to the tarry sweetness of the smoke. He inhaled slowly so as not to burn the back of his throat. His eyes watered slightly and holding his breath, he handed the pipe silently back to Sam.

'All right bro,' said Sam, taking the pipe and lighter. He held the flame to the bowl and drew back until the bud became a little glowing coal. Removing the lighter, he continued to suck. He relit it as the ember dimmed. In two lung-fulls he had emptied the bowl. He tapped it on a tree and refilled it.

'Bro?' he said.

Omar took back the pipe and lit the fresh cone. He took a slightly longer toke this time, and again handed it back to Sam, who speedily hauled the remainder into his lungs.

'Shit mate, I'm fucked now eh,' said Sam hoarsely, tapping the pipe in the same spot on the tree. He pressed the cone into the bark and stared as the hot brass made a small circular mark in the grey bark. 'Fuck me, I'm fucked eh.'

'Fucken eh,' said Omar.

'Fucked,' confirmed Sam. Still, for good measure, he packed another cone and thrust out the pipe. This time Omar stopped drawing on the pipe when his lungs were only half-full, and handed it back to Sam. His brother finished the pipe but with rather less zeal than before. He slowly tapped out the bowl.

'Now I'm fucked. Now I *am* fucked. All right, bro, you done good this morning. That skip mate of yours, he's all right eh.' He looked around at the bush that surrounded them.

As if on cue, a kookaburra began to laugh, somewhere close by. It stopped and some wind rustled through the trees. It was only a slight breeze, but to Omar's ears the purity of the sound made it seem like a thousand snakes hissing. He looked at Sam, who was turning his body a slow 360 degrees. Sam suddenly snapped out of his reverie. 'Let's keep walkin' eh,' he announced. He motioned in a vague direction ahead of them. 'We'll cut through here and see where we get to. I reckon we can go cross-country and find that waterfall, eh? Find it ourselves, eh? Fuck that walking path with all them other suckers on it. We'll go cross-country, eh?'

Sam set off through the gum trees in a direction approximately parallel to the path. As he followed, Omar noticed that they were heading uphill. Soon, they were well into the bush.

'This is fucken all right eh bro?' said Sam, his eyes crinkled, red and rheumy. They looked almost half closed. He strode through the vegetation. 'Check it out, mate, those trees are freakin me out.' He was referring to a large grass tree that stood imposingly a few metres away. 'It's fucken huge eh. It's like a big, burnt pineapple, eh. Like a big bushfire has come through here and left behind all these giant black pineapples. Burnt. Fuck, eh.'

Omar put his fingers up to his eyes. Did they look like Sam's? He hoped not; he hadn't brought any Visine. 'Fucken eh,' he said. 'I dunno ... yeah ... a bushfire, a burnt pineapple, yeah right.'

'Yeah, right, ya stoned cunt! Stop copying everything I say, eh?'

'Ha ha ...' Omar rubbed his eyes again as they kept walking. He could feel his heart thumping in his chest and his tongue seemed swollen and sticky in his mouth. He wished they'd brought some of the Sprite from the picnic. He was still trying to be careful with his Nikes but they were getting scratched and scuffed, especially on the toes and at the side of the heels. Sam had picked up a big stick and was swinging it in front of him like a machete, whipping the crimson tops off some tall wildflowers and lacerating nearby protruding branches whether they impeded his way or not. He continued into the open forest.

Now the terrain seemed to veer slightly steeper to the left and larger rocks appeared on the ground between the vegetation. Sam seemed determined to walk at right angles to the slope. Omar watched his strange limping gait – he looked like that kid nobody talked to at school, the one who had polio when he was a baby. Then he looked down and saw that he himself was walking that way and he laughed out loud.

'Hey bro! Hey bro!' Omar yelled. 'You're walking like a spastic! Hey! Slow down for second eh? Where are we going, anyway?'

Sam stopped and turned. 'I said, we're going to the waterfall. That sign back near the car park said there was a waterfall. So that's where we're going, eh. Look bro, if you want to be a pussy, you can go back to Moma and Bobo. But I'm gonna check out this waterfall by myself, eh? How hard can it be, bro? We're still going in the same direction as that path, yeah?'

'Well ... y'see ... I dunno bro. I don't know. How do we know the path didn't twist around or turn or something, y'know?'

'Fuck! We only been walking for five minutes. How far away could the path be? It can't run away from us. I swear to God, mate, you're a worrier, y'know?'

Omar looked around. The eucalypt trees were all around them. He stepped from side to side and peered between them but couldn't see any evidence of the path. He walked a few metres one way and then in another. He still couldn't make out the snaking, concrete track. 'I think we been walking for more than five minutes, bro.'

'Aw, for fuck's sake, mate, just come for a walk, would ya? We'll find that waterfall and we'll have a piss in it and then we'll go back to Moma and Bobo and tell them what a nice little walkie we had. C'mon bro.'

'Yeah, I'll come. I'm not worried or anything like that. I'm just saying that we been walking out here for more than five minutes, is all. Don't you feel like getting a drink or something?'

'Mate, we can get a drink later. C'mon, it's not gonna kill us. Let's –' Sam stopped and looked behind him. Omar was also staring in the direction of a scrabbling, shuffling noise coming from some bushes a few metres behind Sam.

'What the fuck is that?' said Sam, his eyes widening.

'I dunno,' whispered Omar. They stared at the spot where the sounds emanated from. Dropping his machete-stick, Sam bent down slowly and picked up a rock the size of a cricket ball. Still crouching, he picked up another stone with his free hand.

'Could be a fucken snake, mate. *Fuck*. A fucken snake, mate . . . could be . . . a fucken . . . snake . . . eh?'

Omar continued to stare hard at the spot, trying to make out any serpentine shape in the negative spaces between the leaves and branches. The rustling in the bushes continued. Omar suddenly felt as if he were staring too hard and peeled his eyes away. As he looked around him, a black fuzzy border constrained the edges of his vision, like some kind of binocular effect from a black and white movie. In a few seconds the feeling dissipated and he could see properly again. The rustling continued.

Sam was poised with the rocks in his hands. 'Fuck this for a joke, mate,' he said. 'I'm not waiting here like some stupid cunt, waiting to get chomped on the leg.' With that he hurled one of the rocks towards the source of the sounds. The rock skewed out of his hand and missed the large bush by a good metre. With a cracking, echoing report, the rock hurtled into a small boulder and bounced off. In an instant a small bundle of browny-grey fur shot from the bush and attached itself to the nearest tree trunk. It scurried up the tree, now seemingly more alarmed at its exposure than the sound that had scared it in the first place. Sam's immediate impulse was to throw his other rock towards the animal as hard as he possibly could. To Omar's horror, and against any odds that he would have given, the hurtling stone caught the creature squarely at the back of its furry neck. The horrendous impact seemed to make no sound. The animal dropped from the tree and lay still in some leaves, its four sets of claws pointed at the smattering of blue sky above.

'Fuck! Fuck! Oh my God, I swear! Did you see that, bro? What a fucken shot! Did you check that fucken shot? Fucken *reflexes*, mate! It went like a fucken bullet! What do they call 'em, those bullets in wars and that ... like a fucken tracer bullet! Aw, mate! That was fucken unreal, mate. Bro, fucken bro, did you see that!'

Omar couldn't take his eyes off the soft, dead body on the ground in front of them. The little creature's slightly bulbous eyes were a deep, translucent black-brown. For some reason, Omar thought of strong coffee at the bottom of a shot glass – of espresso coffee, perhaps a macchiato before its dash of milk, or maybe a sweet, potent Turkish brew. Omar looked up at Sam, who was still standing in the spot where he had launched the missile.

'Fucken nailed it, mate. Didn't have a fucken chance! Fucken nailed it! Fucken bam!' He slapped his fist into a palm.

Omar stopped thinking about coffee. He forced himself to look again at the dead possum. Was it dead? He walked towards it and nudged it with a scuffed Nike toe. Through his sneaker he could still feel the softness under the fur, the give of its insides. It wasn't even bleeding or anything. The animal remained motionless.

'Fucken didn't stand a chance bro eh? I'm like a fucken black fella out here, eh? Fucken Aborigine couldn't have done that, eh? Not with a fucken spear, mate. Not even with a fucken gun. Try that with a gun, mate, a fucken shotgun, you fucken couldn't do it in a million years, mate. Not even in the Olympics, mate. Ask the Telopea Street Boys. Aw, mate, that was fucken unbelievable ...'

Sam stayed where he was. Omar stood right above the possum. He studied it, noticing the creamy fur on its belly and the long, skinny tail that ended in a curling, hairless little loop. The animal seemed to stare up at him with a questioning expression. Why? Omar didn't know why. He turned around to look at Sam, who had quietened down somewhat. Now it was Omar's turn to do a slow 360, taking in the forest. Every leaf and branch – every tree seemed to be in sharp relief. He felt like he suddenly had some kind of super-human vision. His thoughts swirled and multiplied in his head as if they were being vitamised in a blender. He had a sudden feeling of being like a blade of grass, of being like a stick or a flower. He looked around at the immense detail contained in the forest around him, and experienced the perception, though it was barely verbal, of the tremendous odds against being born a human being in this world, with so much other stuff around – the trees, the grass, the dirt, the flies, the leaves, this dead possum in front of him with its pink, moist little nose. This was followed by a moment of panic: Don't fucken lose it, mate! That's fucken crazy shit! The admonition was a thought in his own head but it seemed to be Sam's voice he was hearing. Fuck!

'Fuck!' said Sam. 'That little fucken rat-squirrel is fucked. I really fucked it up, eh mate?'

'It's a possum,' said Omar quietly. He forgot what he had just been thinking about, but was uneasy and becoming paranoid. He looked around and noticed how there were very different types of trees. One of the trees had a weird-coloured bark. Nothing around here was one colour. The possum was brown-grey. Its eyes were black-brown. The tree's bark was pink-grey. Fuck! It was peeling off in flakes and it was orange-red underneath! Fuck!

'I hope that thing didn't have kids eh,' said Sam. 'Can't see any little possums around. They'd be in that bush that it ran out from eh?' He looked towards the bush, calmer now. He picked up his machete-stick and moved towards it. He gave it some cursory prods and then a resounding whack, causing it to shiver and shake.

'Nah, no fucken kids in there. Fuck this for a joke, mate. Let's get the fuck out of here. Y'know, that's life eh,' he added, making a movement with his chin towards the dead possum, keeping his eyes on the empty bush. Once again he set off through the under-growth. Omar took one last look at the little ringtail. A small, rusty-coloured ant had discovered the still-warm body and crawled across its forehead. It entered one rounded pink ear. Omar followed Sam, leaving the possum where it lay.

*

They walked on for another half an hour, trampling through plants and stumbling over rocks. The brothers still travelled at a right angle to the slope, though Omar noticed it had a more pronounced gradient.

Sam had rambled a little more about 'nailin' the giant rat, but had then quietened down again. Sometimes he muttered a curse or an oath after being scratched by a branch or tripping over uneven ground. He was particularly incensed after stepping into the dung of some unidentified animal.

'Probably a kangaroo shit eh,' Omar volunteered, looking at the pebbly little stools as Sam scraped and stabbed at the tread on his sneakers with his machete-stick.

'Fucken kangaroo, mate! I'll fucken brain him if I see him!' promised Sam, brandishing his weapon. 'It's like that Bugs Bunny cartoon, eh, where they think that baby kangaroo is a big mouse, eh?'

'Ha ha! Yosemite Sam!' said Omar.

'I'll fucken nail that fucker if I see him, I swear to God!' said Sam. 'Give me a fucken rock and I'll fucken nail him, mate. Just one shot. Bam!' His eyes scanned the ground for projectiles, just in case.

They walked on. Omar continued to follow, mostly avoiding the scrapes and pitfalls endured by his brother. However, he couldn't avoid dung on his shoes and longed to get home to scrape out the treads and run them under some water. His head was clearing a bit and he hadn't thought too much about the killing of the possum.

Suddenly Sam stopped and listened for a moment. He moved forward again, this time with the slope. Omar stopped too, thinking that maybe Sam could hear the sound of running water.

'I fucken told you, bro! Hear that! I fucken told you, bro!' Sam jogged down the slope. Omar had no choice but to follow.

They jogged downhill, gaining momentum as they went, hurdling small boulders, Sam giving exuberant whoops as he did so. Then Omar saw a little splash of colour ahead. A red cap, worn by a small child in a pram. The child, who might have been one or two years old, was crying. A dumpy and bothered-looking young mother was pushing the pram. The father trudged ahead, lugging an esky and picnic basket, his ponderous, exposed calves like two upended pink jeroboams.

Omar and Sam had rejoined the path.

'I fucken told you, bro!' repeated Sam.

Omar wasn't sure what all the fuss was about. 'Yeah … but I thought … we was gonna get to the waterfall cross-country. Y'know?'

'What do you fucken think that sign says?' said Sam, pointing to a wooden signpost. In faded, etched letters it read: McKenzie Falls 400 m. Warning: Steep Path. Up ahead of the sign there was a fork in the path. On one side the concrete continued to snake its way ahead, keeping loosely parallel with the creek. To the left of this was a dirt track that led to the falls.

They stood for a minute, regaining their breath.

'Fucken as good as, mate,' said Sam. 'As fucken good as going cross-country, mate. Don't forget you got to see all that nature and everything. These suckers here, like this loser …' he motioned to the man who carried his family's picnic, '… didn't see nothing, did they? Just followed the path. Fucken dopey cunts, mate.'

'So shall we keep going? It'll take us a while to get up that path. It says it's pretty steep so we should go now so we can check it out and get back before Moma and Bobo want to leave, y'know. Let's get up there and have a ciggie at the top and then we'll come down, eh?'

Sam stood staring at the sign. 'You know what, bro, fuck it. Let's not fucken go up to see that stupid fucken waterfall. I can't be fucken bothered, mate. I'm already all sweaty and my shoes, look at 'em, mate, they're covered in shit. Plus I'm fucken thirsty too, eh. C'mon, let's go back to where Moma and Bobo are.' Reaching into his pocket for ciggies, he stalked off in the other direction. Omar looked back in the direction of the waterfall and then turned on his heel.

'Give us a ciggie then,' he called out to Sam, as he began to follow him back to the family picnic.

The Last Cheese

A M Sladdin

The rosy lens of my hindsight is not curative to the dyslexia of my mismatched affections. I am catatonic. I quake here and rail. Underneath my lamentation, however, there is the kernel of new beginning. Fresh hope. Unfetteredness is near, yet I stumble, unsure of plotting my own course. My shackles are still here to slough off if I can gather the volition.

Just now my body plays fox on me: with cell-memory on permanent flashback, my past's pain assails me. Incapacitated, it seems, nevertheless, that I must perform some belated exorcism to allow any future success. The house is disorganised. The dishes reek in the sink. The clean clothes crumple and are strewn with cat hairs waiting on the bed near their proper housing. Other cupboards bulge with the nostalgic relics of my nearly unlived life. These cards and letters from others press heaviest, along with scraps of scavenged rock and dusty beached coral corpses.

I suspect my dread at collating this collection, this detritus of my life, of making myself the small sum of these fragments, is what has effectively stymied me. A bulging catastrophe awaits attention in each room. The chaos sets a precedent for the other over-looked projects: my unwritten writing, my unfinished paintings, my unset gemstones and, ultimately, my unstretched womb.

And why? Because of my denial. I don't want to own my too-fleeting life, my wasted time or my wasting talents. Apparently I lack the gumption to pull myself out of this spiral. Instead I keep on heading for the gurgler. Down, down. And having blundered into this whirlpool I must tread water Red-Queen furiously just to stay put. I may flounder if I swim against the rip, yet if I trust it, if I am able to surrender my pride and fears, I will survive to be deposited on a fresh Eden's beach of new potential. Therefore, like any drowning insect, as I flail I do look up and out at the world beyond my myopic circuit, past the small wake of my repetitious tread, and hope to rejoin a larger and livelier project. Live a bigger life.

Am I as blameless for my demise as a hapless blundering insect? It seems that the continuum of my despair is dictated by myself. For while it may have been accidental, that first crash into a glassy-eyed abyss, I now curtail myself with the concept of incapacity. In a Wildean way: perhaps the first night, or week, or month, or year, of being drug-fucked may have been mere misfortune but, surely, the decade is missing through indifference alone. And what the resultant self-aggrandisement and petty jealousies have given me, proves no buoy.

Instead my self, my actual yet long-absent self, is weighed down by these unreal projections. Time spent on possible glory and real and imagined slights, a long time, is gone. Phut! The longer I cogitate on my projects – I'll write x, I'll paint y – the less time I have to realise any of them. I am getting like Malone anchored a'bed and grubbing for my pencil end; soon there will not be enough physical time left to do many or any of them. Will I bother or will I sit here, stunned-mullet silent and still, and fritter away the rest of my life as well? Will I produce any work? Any children?

This unattractive option of victimhood – what is its appeal to me? That I can pretend blamelessness for my own failings? Failure? I can find a plethora of scapegoats for my own failure to thrive. There are many won'ts that I employ to disguise my own lack of will. He won't . . . she won't . . . rather than I will. What solace has my self-medication afforded me? More and more self-forgetfulness: my nearly-lived life. It seemed preferable to owning my self, my life, through remembrance. Though to succeed I will have to emulate my sister's total self-forgetfulness and achieve death too.

What though of love? Is that not an attractive enough prospect to encourage endeavour? To keep me swimming? I've heard of that lifeboat, love, and have felt its distant wake but I do not call to it from my whirlpool. It seems I fear further piracy.

Do you know of Mrs Pepperpot? She starred in my favourite book as a child. Intermittently, she would shrink as tiny as a pepper pot. In hindsight, her husband didn't, yet he was called Pepperpot too, I think. In the story Mr P made a fantastic front door, beautifully crafted and painted a shiny green, to secure their house before they made the long annual journey to market to sell their cheese, for their yearly income. Fear that robbers will wreck the door has the peculiar couple leave it unlocked. But, with further stupid consideration, the pair decide robbers are likely to break it down anyway, expecting it to be locked. God knows why, when they'd gotten it off its hinges, they didn't merely lean it on the wall and proceed to market. Perhaps it didn't occur to them. So off they set, Mr P bent double carrying the door with the three large disks of cheese on top of it, and, of course, shrunk tiny and sitting on one was Mrs Pepperpot navigating for him.

On and on they toiled. And, as they reached the foot of the mountain, they went up and up. Disastrously and suddenly, one of the cheeses rolled from the door and bounced away, down the slope of the mountain. I do not recall, although I now seemingly favour apportioning blame, whose bright idea it was to throw the second cheese down. Mr or Mrs P's? The rationale was that the second cheese would bounce and land close to the other and then both would be recovered. A little risky, true, but it must have appeared more reasonable to them than cutting their income by a third in accepting the loss of the first cheese. Down rolling went the second. And it went missing too. There remain the unhappy couple, as I recall the tale, wondering whether to cast the final cheese down the hillside and thus possibly recover all three, or to accept their losses and be content with the one remainder.

This is also the story, now, of the small return of my investments in love. In particular, the one I have chosen to love. My baggage, my door – on which I suspend my cheesy trio of faith, love and sur-render – is built from childhood terror flanked by the thick planks of addiction's denial. My heart and body leapt from this wooden podium and rolled to him of their own accord. My game first cheese leapt unheralded and unexpectedly towards him. I followed it, despite his vacant reception, with portions of the second. I threw them down willingly. Love. Affection. Understanding. Compassion. Empathy. My body. I threw in housework, gardening and endless hostessing. I had decided to play house my whole life. It suited me to be bunkered down, and his imperviousness didn't have a patch on my own.

I also threw in my goals and creativity. I concede, now, that the gully never said Throw more cheese! It was my own reckless folly. I considered that the more I threw, like the Pepperpots, the more likely I was to reap a final reward. Instead I, too, was left with less.

And here is my similarly unhappy non-ending: will I throw my last reserves of time and affection here? Where it has proven quite profitless? Will I keep my reserves unto me or will I throw them to the precipice of his indifference, hoping to fill the gaps, his incline, and recoup all that may be lost?

Presence

Rebecca Ebert

Sweating kelpie strains at the rope
Rubbing a groove into his neck
Pulling his head out past the cab
To feel the wind rush past his face.
Farmer follows the southern fence,
Searching for the fly-blown sheep he'd
Seen decomposing from the road.

Black flies buzz around the head as
Ants march into empty eye-sockets
Left bare by crows that dig out the eyes
Of dying sheep and newborn lambs.

The farmer takes the jerry, and
Liberally anoints the sunken frame,
Petrol soaks the matted wool before
Flames consume the unsightly corpse.

Kelpie skips around the burning sheep,
Dancing to the smells and sounds
Of bubbling fat and char-grilled meat.
And the farmer stands as witness
To the bush cremation at his feet.

The Gift

Gillian Britton

Stella's bathrobe is no longer white. It has yellowed in the 18 months since Sammy's birth, like teeth, battered by exposure and the constancy of function. She has made coffee, but she doesn't drink it. She is listening to Sammy, who is wired, having slept only three full hours through the night. She can picture him, upright on his little sprung legs, rattling like a zoo animal on the rails of his cot. He is calling her, in the only way he can: little grunts and shrill hooting. She can't answer, not yet. She grasps her coffee mug, one palm across its warm, steaming mouth. Not yet, she thinks, not yet. And then he falls silent, and she breathes.

Later, Tony struts in, trailing his odours and his early morning spruceness.

'His nappy needed changing,' he says, 'I did it for you.'

She could remind him that it is the first time in weeks that he has changed a nappy. Hardly something worth strutting over. But she doesn't say it. He is wearing his grey suit and the purple Christmas-party tie. He is whistling, as he has taken to doing of late, departing from them with his assertions of cheeriness. Flaunting his liberty. He has his role in their colluded disaster: to leave promptly at 8:05 each morning and frolic about in his bread-winning capacity until he arrives home for dinner and a dutiful 15 minutes with Sammy before declaring it bed-time. Not that he puts Sammy to bed. That is outside of his domain. Only Stella can manage getting Sammy to sleep. She's mastered it. A hell of a task. Takes hours some nights.

He pours himself a coffee. He looks at Stella, who is silent. He doesn't want to ask.

'I've been up half the night with him,' she says.

'Really?' he says, 'I never heard you.' And then, 'You should have woken me.'

She doesn't bother with a reply. He gulps coffee, tugs at his tie.

'I'll be late tonight,' he says. 'Office *do*.' He rolls the word, in anticipation. She rolls her eyes, but keeps them square in front of her, out of his range. He knows the look anyway – they do this often enough.

'If you're not going back to work, Stella,' he trots out the mandatory justification, 'I have no choice but to crawl up the boss's arse.'

'*Choice*?' she says. 'Who said anything about *choice*? What am *I* choosing here? Am I extending my vacation in the Greek Islands, for God's sake? I didn't *expect* it to happen this way. I didn't *expect* not to go back to work.'

He holds his hands up, wards her off.

'I'm not having this conversation right now,' he says, 'I'm only reminding you that someone around here has to pay the mortgage.'

'And I've chosen to sit around here in my bathrobe all day?' She holds on to her coffee. She says the words to the wall.

'That's the way you've chosen to handle it, yes,' he says. Now she is watching him. Her jaw aches. She hates the smell of him. The thickness of his neck garrotted in its stiff white collar. He throws the remains of his coffee in the sink, takes a slug of water from the tap, strains his tie up one more notch.

She stands up. She has a white-knuckle grip on the table.

'What else am I supposed to do?' she says. 'You tell me.'

She doesn't scream. In fact, she whispers. But the scream is implied. He is standing, hands still on the noose, looking across at her. His eyes have that telltale bulging. The vein on his left temple visibly pulsates. She sees what he is seeing – her bathrobe hanging like loose flesh. He is watching the loose yellow flesh of his wife, when the noise of his son's freakish squawking begins again from the other room.

He turns away from her, brushing at his suit. He leans on the sink and stares into the banal back yard.

'I didn't choose this either,' he says, finally. Sammy's squealing fills the silent space between them.

Sesame Street is on. Not that Sammy watches, but the noises are friendly. Stella has left him in the pen (no one uses such a thing these days, but Stella is grateful for it) in order to have a shower. He is working against the rails, like a small caged beast, barking and howling as she comes back, in her bathrobe, her hair wrapped in a towel. He doesn't look at her – they are not sure exactly what he can see – but he knows she is there; he begins to grunt. She watches his jaws mashing at sounds, jaws that seem to jut from shoulders because there is no neck in Sammy's case. He has an eyebrow that spreads across the entire length of his forehead like a sleazy, misplaced moustache. He has eyes submerged in hooded, bruised pockets and do not see the world in the way of the normal, the blessed. She steels herself to see him as others do; this is a daily penance. To never forget the raw gift of Sammy, the imperfect, which shattered her naive belief that the circumstances of the normal, the blessed, are ordered, are under one's privileged control.

She lifts him from the pen. He stiffens, as he always does. She feels the board of his torso, the desperately flailing limbs, but she holds him against her anyway. He may grow used to it. This she longs for more than anything, to feel him soften, to feel the small-ness of him curving into her. She feels the drawing in her breasts, the tingling of her nipples at the thought of this, but Sammy grunts and squirms his body from her; the tiny pins of his legs hit the floor and he propels himself, anywhere – the destination is not important. The TV is an obstacle; he flattens himself against it. Elmo, cute and furry, dances around under Sammy's spread-eagled arms and she wonders what he sees.

'It's Elmo, Sammy,' she says. He grunts. He pumps his legs, lunging like a squat prima donna and then he is off again. She watches Elmo dance. She wants not to watch Sammy. She wants not to have to chase him. But he is running down the hallway now and she wills herself to stand and follow. And what will happen when he is older, she thinks, as she plucks up the sparrow light-ness of him, and she can no longer save him from the danger of himself?

She puts him back in the pen. He screams.

'I'm ignoring you, Sammy,' she says, and walks away down the hall, the violence of his screaming hurling knives at the muscles of her neck. She makes a decision, and goes back to him. She switches on the overhead fluoro. She is not supposed to do this. Professionals do not advise it. Just for a minute, she tells herself, just while I get dressed. He is quiet, instantly. He lies on his back. He brings his hand up to his eyes and begins to flick. He makes noises of pleasure, flicking his fingers in front of his face in a miasma of fascination.

She goes to get dressed, because it is necessary. They are going to go shopping, she has decided. They are going to go shopping because they need things. They are going to go shopping because she cannot bear the gaping hole of hours. Because she hasn't the will to engage him, not today. She hasn't the heart to coax and cajole him into responsiveness. She thinks of all the virtuous activities prescribed by the speech pathologist and the physiotherapist and the child psychologist and she thinks of her bed, and the warm fug of it, and the best that she can do is get dressed.

She puts on the grey tracksuit pants. She wears them every day. She considers the jeans (since she is going out, and she used to have some pride) but she can't stand their tight chaffing, the reminder of the excess bulk of her thighs and stomach, which require a gym or early morning jogging, she knows, but she can't think about it. Tony would call it a *choice*. He looks at her thighs and she knows what he would think. He stops at the gym three nights a week on his way home from work. He doesn't necessarily *want* to – it's a matter of discipline. She could get an exercise bike. She could eat less. But she is increasingly attached to eating. It is pure pleasure. It is a quick fix. She would not admit this, and she is ashamed of it, but the shame itself is part of why she does it. She puts on the grey tracksuit pants and her long black jumper. She begins to pull back her hair, but this requires a mirror and she is not up to it, not today, so she gives up.

Playschool is just starting: 'Open wide, come inside'. She is flooded with an odd nostalgia. For what? Certainly not her own childhood. Is it possible to feel nostalgia for what you might have wished for? For what will never be?

Sammy is still on his back. Still flicking. He has dirtied his nappy. She can smell it. She steels herself, turns off the fluoro. Instantly he is on his feet, screaming.

'Come on, Sammy boy,' she goes to lift him, but the nappy, too loose, is seeping. He begins his knee bends, in anticipation of being lifted.

'No way,' she says, 'not until I clean you up.'

He shrieks.

'Ma Ma Ma Ma,' the sounds fall from his mouth and she stops.

'What did you say?' She goes back to him. She grips his hands. 'Did you say what I think you said? Did you say Mama, Sammy boy, Mama?'

Sammy goes on shrieking, but she is jubilant; he might speak. All the professionals were hedging their bets; nobody seemed to have a clue what he was capable of and so they fed her a strict diet of doom and worst-case scenarios. But what if they were wrong? What if Sammy were to prove them all wrong?

She walks to the bathroom, grabs wipes and a clean nappy, and indulges herself, gorging on this small quiver of hope. She spends a moment in a fabricated future in which Sammy, due no doubt to her tireless efforts, is a risen star in the galaxy of normality. She imagines the face, unfolded; the hair, which is his best feature, strong and dark about his face; the stocky adolescent form. She imagines a smile that betrays a modicum of self-awareness and compounded human knowledge. She does not let herself become cliched or fanciful – she does not dress him in the garb of graduation, espousing witticisms from the podium to an adoring crowd. But she does allow herself the glimmer of that smile, the feel of his body, once a torment of incomprehension, now supple in its responsiveness.

'My little star,' she says, walking back to him.

She wipes at his legs.

'Say "Mama",' she says to him, '"Mama, Mama",' as she wipes, and reaches in to claim him, and all the time he screams in his strange, barking way, and he arches, as she lifts, becoming a wash-board. She pulls his body in, but his head defies her, arcing away, the hand planted firmly in front of it; the miasma of flicking. She places him on the rug, pulls his hand away and he screams.

'Sammy,' she says, turning his face to look at her, but his eyes scatter. 'Sammy,' she says, 'we're going shopping.'

*

It isn't raining, but there is the intimation of damp, the sky no more than an offering of spent cloud, off-colour and mooning. She navigates the car through grey, while Sammy, stiff in his car seat, batters his head from side to side and wails a belligerent protest at the outrage of motion. She turns the radio on, and he quietens, his hand moving in front of his face. Hits from the 80s and 90s. She sings along. She beats time on the steering wheel. They glide along through the impetus of grey, one car in an ocean of intention-borne traffic; she feeds on the utter monotony of it.

She parks the car, pulls the pram from the hatch and pulls him from his seat. He begins to scream as soon as he is in. She decides she cannot bear it. She lifts him out, struggles to fold the pram and push it back into the hatch and still he screams. She walks the steep ascent from the car park with him in her arms. She attempts to hold him to her, to whisper to him, to distract him in the way that mothers can, through gentle, Siren-like persuasion, but Sammy is having none of it. He arches away from her; she pulls him in harder to stop him falling. He jogs against her, small jockey legs pressed to canter, and then whoops a series of incantations, like the eerie noises of large moonlit birds. She gives in and lets him down, aware of the looks of ordinary strangers. She sets her veneer of calm against them. Sammy rushes on ahead of her, down the sloping length of the mall. She picks up her pace and she watches him, noting from this distance the ghoulish curiosity of these strangers, who stare openly at him now: ugly, neck-less boy, cavorting outside the reach of his mother's cosseting. She runs then, catches him up, swings him, all swooping kisses, into the framework of the trolley, and heads in.

Once they are inside the supermarket, he is quiet. He always is – it is the flickering of the overhead fluoros, which he watches through his own flickering fingers. She slows her pace. She feels her own breathing. This is why she shops; for 30 minutes in the space of her own mind. She doesn't think about what they need. She scans shelves and buys what leaps at her. It pisses Tony off, this random buying, but her mind is not on shopping, it is on breathing, taking in silence like water.

*

She had known the day he was born.

'What's wrong with him?' she'd asked, holding the strange bird of him.

'Nothing's wrong with him.' The family had laughed at her. 'He's just like Tony – ugly as sin.'

Nurses had seemed to scurry away from her, busying themselves with other patients, and Tony had paced at the foot of the bed, talking into his mobile, calling everybody, telling everybody: 'It's a boy, Samuel Anthony, five-pound three-ounces. Tiny, but healthy.'

Only Stella, nursing the awkward limbs of Sammy, watching the back of Tony and the busyness of nurses, had known. Her knowing had become a bubble – clinging to Sammy, she had floated beyond the reach of them, to where their voices could not follow, into the isolation of hopeless love and the ravenous gorging of regret.

Doctors began appearing by day three. Syndromes were suggested, but no conclusive diagnosis had yet been offered. So many hours and days of testing over 18 months and nobody knew. Autism, of course, but there was more than that. Nobody could tell her how far from normal he would be, and so she had watched and hoped. Sammy had grown and crawled and walked, but in no other way seemed to identify with the world. The family gradually gave up their pretence and stopped gushing at him. Grandmothers were dutiful about knitting and providing, but nobody could hold him – it was like cuddling a galah. They all avoided it, even Tony. Especially Tony.

She is staring at cereal boxes, all neatly lined. Of course, she thinks, he will leave us. She hates him, because he can. He has *choices*. She hates herself, because in this moment she envies him. And then, she thinks, lifting Weet-Bix into the trolley, We are alone anyway, so what is the difference?

The moment she exits the supermarket, Sammy begins to grunt and climb. She pushes him back in but he squeals, his head beginning its dance of topsy-turvy. She pins him in the trolley seat.

'No, no, no,' she wheedles as she pushes. And then she hears it. 'Stella?' With a question mark.

She turns. 'Mary.' She laughs. She swallows panic.

Mary tries to hug her, but Sammy is grunting his way higher and higher out of the seat. She turns away to pull him out. Mary's own boy sits placid in the trolley, staring at Sammy, who is making the noises of a wild animal.

'He hates shopping,' Stella laughs.

But Mary's eyes are on Stella, not Sammy.

'Why are you not returning my calls?' she asks.

'Oh,' Stella laughs again, 'I just seem to be so busy, you know how it is.'

Mary is shaking her head.

'No,' she says, 'Stella, no more. We've been friends for too long. Don't do this.'

Sammy is inching his way down her side. He hits the ground and takes off.

'I have to go,' she says, snatching at her trolley and heading towards Sammy, who is headed for the entrance. She doesn't turn around. She doesn't want to see them watching. Mary of all people, with her perfect boy.

The automatic doors part obligingly in response to Sammy's light feet. Open wide, it's *Playschool*. Stella pushes the trolley through behind him. It is raining without ambivalence now; the world is drowning. And there is nobody there to help, suddenly, as if the humanity of the mall has sealed itself off from them, ushering them into oblivion. The only sign of life is one moving car, its reverse lights red-blood beacons in the slash of rain, and Sammy, victim to his only fascination, running towards them.

'Sammy!' she screams into the rain. Making the only choice available to her, she lets go of her laden trolley and runs to snatch him. She pulls him into her arms, wraps him in the coat of her, against the blight of rain and death and then turns to see the trolley begins its descent. Slow waltz and gathering speed, it hurls itself at the sides of parked cars, battering at each in succession with its dead weight before it flips itself over the final frontier of gutter, spewing its contents like whale spume into the neatness of pine-bark and shrub.

What, she asks herself, is she supposed to do now?

She sinks down on her knees, onto the bitumen, still holding Sammy. Tears that she is barely aware of meld into the gunfire of rain. She rocks the non-compliant body of her son, who sees nothing past his hand, which he begins to flick now, inches from his face.

Held from behind in this way she can touch him. She can hold her face close to the strength of his dark hair. She can smell the odour that belongs only to him, to Sammy.

'Mama,' she says, her mouth at his ear. 'Mama,' she says again.

Bad Tailor

A M Sladdin

Scrap heap
The story of a remnant
My fabric is rent now
Torn off the bolt
Trodden underfoot by the yard.

He glibly scissored through me
Not following a fitting pattern.
Allowing no ease in my seat
Like a pair of ill-made
Op-shop trousers
No give in the arse.
He picked apart my tangled heart
But threw the threads away.

Although my whole yardage was once sufficient
to cover love
my pretty remnant scraps
now fill a ragbag
and
this is not an age of patchworkers.

What Was and Is and Shall Not Be

Heather Taylor Johnson

There were other days
when like some fluorescent kite
pink from sun and yellowed hair
I swayed with rushes
and lost my stomach
and laughed and ran,
threw sand with my toes
and swam until I seeped out salt.

And there was a man,

who built with me dreams of densely watered dirt
and sat beside me, sharing stories from shells
and we held the world between the hairs of our skin
that smelled of sweet coconut sweat.

This place was a water-coloured picture book.
This place was fish and chips.

But I was younger,

knew what to do with what I had,
I knew the taste of a sun-screened man,
knew how to take off my clothes,
run 'til I fell
and splash and dive
and swim.

Ten years later

this place is darker
and I could mean the clouds
or the overall feel
because there's something about metal cranes
and concrete stacks in the distance of my ocean
or the beach that's not sand but boulders
the size of my weakened back
when it's slouched in gloomy defeat.

This place is starving seagulls.

I could just be brooding
because my spectrum of sky is grey to dark grey,
because I'm older and I get this way,
alone and extinguished,
cold and alone.

This place is for sinking stones

as small as these tied to each finger and toe
or those that dangle from both my ears
or as large as the one that hangs from my neck
or the one that cuts my wrists.

The Investigation

Petra Fromm

Booker was sitting on a time bomb. Actually, since the room wasn't much bigger than a cupboard and there was nowhere else to sit, he was sitting on the photocopier. The bomb was inside the copier, connected by a snarl of coloured wires to one of those old-fashioned alarm clocks with two bells on top. The room was otherwise empty except for a waste-basket containing a single, crumpled piece of paper; the walls were completely bare, and in spite of Occupational Health and Safety Regulations, there was no smoke alarm or sprinkler.

Booker salvaged the paper, flattening out the creases. It was a photocopy of some sheila's arse. She was wearing a g-string that said 'grin 'n' bear it' along the band. It wasn't really evidence, but Booker wrote a memo of it in his notepad. Then, with nothing better to do, he closed his eyes and waited for his life to flash before them. Nothing happened. When he opened his eyes, he realised he was sharing the limited space in the copy room with a stranger.

'Fuck me drunk! Where the hell did you come from?'

'Where I come from there's no such place as hell,' the stranger replied morosely. 'No sex or booze either, more's the pity.'

Booker felt his heart stop. 'Are you Death?'

'No. Although, apart from the halitosis, he's not a bad bloke. I'm assigned to the Investigations Branch.' The stranger removed his hat, looked for somewhere to hang it, and placed it carefully on a brass hook on the wall. From the right-hand pocket of his coat, he removed a small notepad and a ballpoint pen. 'Would you mind answering a few questions? It won't take long,' he asked Booker.

Booker couldn't think of anything to say, so he closed his mouth.

'Right then. Let's start with your full name and date of birth shall we?'

'Um. My name's Gerald Thomas Booker. I was born on September 14th, 1963. I'm 39. My birthday's next week – they say that life begins at 40.'

'Maybe, but not yours mate.'

'What's that supposed to mean?'

'I would have thought it was obvious. Isn't that a bomb you're sitting on?' The Investigator pointed to the copier. 'Mind if I call you Gerry?'

Booker was having trouble keeping up. He shook his head, trying to clear his thoughts.

'Great.' The Investigator resumed his pose, pen hovering above the notepad. 'So Gerry, briefly describe the circumstances leading up to your imminent demise.'

More from habit than anything else, Booker assumed debriefing mode: 'Well, I'm a cop. I was recently assigned to the investigation of an alleged terrorist group. I received information that one of the secretaries here was having it off with the principal suspect. I thought I'd ask her a few questions, and by a strange coincidence, interrupted the perpetrators planting the bomb. I managed to slip out of sight long enough to give my mate Randy, in the bomb squad, a call. Unfortunately, the offenders found me before I could give him the exact location. Anyway, they grabbed my phone and shoved me in here. You can't see the bomb, but there's a timer in the paper tray.' Booker pointed to the clock. 'Look, it's set to go off at 4:30.'

The Investigator glanced obligingly at the clock. 'So why don't you disconnect the timer? You know, just rip the wiring out?'

'Because the bloody thing will go off! Disarming a bomb is specialist work, not something you can just fuck about with. Have you got any more stupid questions?'

'Take it easy, Gerry. No need to get the shits up, I'm almost done.' The Investigator eyeballed his notepad. 'Where was I? Ah, yes. Is there anything, or anyone for that matter, keeping you here? You know, if you were to die now, would you have any unfinished business?'

Booker shrugged; he liked to keep things simple. 'No, not really. Well, my mate Randy would probably be sorry to see me go, but he wouldn't be inconsolable. We don't call him Randy for nothing. The office knows who the terrorists are, and we have enough evidence to charge them. I wouldn't mind seeing them convicted, but apart from that, I haven't been assigned another case.'

The Investigator shook his head. 'Bit of a shame that. Okay, just one last question. What do you think will happen to you after you die?'

'What?' Booker gazed at the Investigator vaguely. 'I really couldn't say. Never given it much thought. I'm not religious, if that's what you mean?'

'Well, that's it then. Just bear with me a moment, will you?' The Investigator took what looked like a calculator from the left-hand pocket of his coat and pushed a few buttons. 'Oh dear,' he muttered at the readout. 'I'll start again.' He pushed a few more buttons but seemed no happier with the result.

'Gerry, there's no easy way to break it to you: according to my calculations, you don't qualify for an afterlife.'

'What! Why the hell not?' Booker jumped off the copier and tried, unsuccessfully, to pace the room. 'Try that thing again, you probably made a mistake.'

'I've already done it twice, and I'm afraid there's been no mistake. The problem lies in that you have no soul. You know, those R and B wowsers sing about it all the time. See, the thing about Life is that you're supposed to get involved. One way or another, you only get an afterlife if you have some unfinished business. And you don't, you said so yourself. If it makes you feel better, you could even call it time off for good behaviour.'

Booker wondered if this was Randy's idea of a joke, maybe instead of a stripper-gram for his birthday? No, Randy always sent a stripper-gram.

'I'm not sure I understand.' He screwed his face up at the Investigator. 'Shouldn't I have been notified or something?'

'Never mind.' The Investigator was suddenly cheerful. 'The good news is there's still a bit of time left before the bomb goes off. Do you play cards?'

Booker nodded. The Investigator took an impossible three steps backwards and, with a flourish, exposed a tall storage cabinet. 'Here's one I prepared earlier.'

'You're not funny,' said Booker, more depressed than amazed.

'Yes, I am. You've just got a shithouse sense of humour.' But the Investigator stopped grinning and opened the cabinet. Inside was a folding card table and two of those tiny stools designed for golfers. Unfolding the table and setting out the chairs only took a minute.

'We may as well get comfy eh?' Winking at Booker, he reached into the top shelf of the cabinet and removed a bottle of single-malt whisky, a compact wooden box of cigars and a deck of cards. He arranged them on the table, searched a pocket for Redheads and dropped them on the cigar box with a shrug. 'No glasses, we'll have to drink out of the bottle.'

Booker reached for the whisky, letting it let trickle past his lips and over his tongue. He was hungry and knew he probably shouldn't drink it straight on an empty stomach. Normally, he would have had a steak sandwich for lunch, but not today. A steak sandwich with the lot, no egg. Eggs tasted all right, but the yellow put him off. Last month, an American CIA guy was sent over to advise the boss on terrorist tactics and he'd raved on about meatball sandwiches and jelly doughnuts. Booker didn't get it. What was wrong with a steak sandwich, or even a Chicko roll? His stomach growled as the Investigator dealt two piles of cards on the table.

'Right then. Poker?' the Investigator asked, wriggling his eyebrows at Booker.

*

Booker lost three hands in a row.

'See?' The Investigator jabbed his cigar at Booker. 'That's your problem, right there. You play poker the same way you play

Life. Couldn't bluff to save yourself. You're just not a risk-taker are you?'

'What do you mean? I took a risk pursuing those terrorists, didn't I?'

'That's just your job. I'm talking about Life. Life with a capital L. Let me give you an example. Remember that gorgeous sheila in high school? You really fancied her, didn't you? And she liked you. But did you ever ask her out? No, course not. You were too shit-scared that she'd say no, maybe even more scared of what might happen if she didn't. And what's worse is that you're too dense to regret it.'

Booker dredged his memory. 'Oh yeah, Angela Prescott; she was a bit of all right. Do you mean she would've said yes?'

'You're missing the point, son.' The Investigator shook his head in vague disappointment, reminding Booker of the time he backed over the letterbox and had to come clean to his father. He took another contemplative swig from the bottle, relishing the bite of the whisky. This time it bypassed his stomach and swam round his knees.

'My father always told me to know my limitations.'

'Yes. He also told you to lay off the booze. Did you listen?'

Booker slid the bottle back onto the table. 'So how did Angela Prescott end up anyway?'

'Don't you know? She married the school footy hero; his name escapes me at the moment. You know, though, he played AFL for a while, died last year, in a brawl at St Kilda.'

'I know who you mean. I'm surprised she married him though. He was a complete wanker.'

'Yeah, so she discovered. Still, he's doing quite well in therapy.'

'What, you mean he got an afterlife? He was an arsehole!' Booker felt like kicking the photocopier in the guts. 'You're telling me that there is an afterlife, but I don't qualify because I'm what . . . mediocre?'

'In a word, yes.'

'And you call that justice?'

'No mate, I don't. It's no good whingeing; it's not about worldly concepts of justice. Anyway, I don't make the rules. I just do the paperwork. You have to try and understand. It's not that you've been corrupt; it's not about crime and punishment per se. To merit an afterlife you have to become meaningfully involved in the process of living. Now that I think about it, it should be a crime for anyone to be as disinterested in Life as you are. You've never worried about dying because you've got bugger all to live for. Be honest, you don't really give a toss about an afterlife. You're just pissed off because you can't have one. Think about it.'

Booker thought. He could feel his brain trying to nut out a convincing defence, but the whisky assured him it wasn't important; it could wait until tomorrow.

The Investigator was shaking his head again. 'See what I mean? Look, let's not fuck about. I still have to read you your rights and take a short statement. We're running out of time.'

'You never know, maybe the bomb squad will get here?'

'Doubtful. They've got their hands full evacuating the area. Otherwise, when the bomb goes off, there will be a disaster. Probably hundreds killed. In fact, now you're being a bit selfish. Aren't you?' The Investigator's near-black eyes pinned Booker to the copier.

'Possibly.' Booker faltered, then rallied. 'But if I hadn't been doing my job properly no one would know about the bomb. I may not have stopped the terrorists, but I gave everyone enough warning to get out. After all, I'm the poor bastard getting blown up. Surely I get some credit for that?'

'Undoubtedly. They'll award you with a medal for bravery. Posthumously, of course.'

'What about a reprieve? I could reform, be more interesting, more involved. Would that make a difference?'

'Unlikely, given your past record. I mean, it's just not your style, is it?'

Booker's stomach growled in panic as the whisky threatened to come back up. 'Can't you do something to help me? Please?'

'I don't know Gerry,' the Investigator sighed. 'Maybe they have been a bit hard on you.' Sniffing, he wiped his nose on the back of his coat sleeve. 'It's against recommended procedure, but I suppose I could have a word with the Super. I don't fancy your chances though.' He took a mobile phone from the inside breast pocket of his coat. 'And before you ask, no, you can't use this phone to ring your mate; it's a privileged line. Don't worry though, this should only take a few minutes.'

Booker looked at the timer. 'That's about all I've got left.' He waited, cracking his knuckles one at a time.

The Investigator pressed the speed dial. 'Sorry,' he shrugged. 'I've been placed in a queue.'

Booker closed his eyes and tried to pray. Instead, Angela Prescott came to mind. Strange really, how he hadn't thought about her in years; there was a time when he'd thought of nothing else. She wasn't exactly beautiful, sort of pink and fluffy, playful and trusting. Like a kitten. She had a way of looking up at a bloke that made him feel, well, big. And now she was a widow. He suddenly wished he'd asked her out. It might have saved her from a shithouse marriage, and him from being condemned to oblivion. He wondered vaguely what life might have been like with someone to come home to.

When Booker opened his eyes, he was alone in the room. There was no sign of the Investigator. A glance at the timer confirmed there were four minutes and 59 seconds before the bomb went off. The door shuddered. Someone was pounding on the other side and he heard Randy yell his name.

'Booker! Mate, are you in there? Get out of the way, we're gonna break the door down!'

The blade of an axe sliced through a panel of the door as Booker crouched beside the copier and waited.

Self-Editing

Ilona Merckenschlager

Sarah had 20 pairs of custom-made brogues lining her wardrobe. It wasn't that she particularly liked the style. In fact her whims extended far beyond their cloddishness. Sarah loved fashionable footwear. So much so that she had been a subscriber to *Shoe In*, the vogue magazine of footwear, for years. She would gaze longingly at the strappy little bits of string and leather perched on ridiculously high heels, and sigh with envy. She noticed feet everywhere she went. The smooth high arches, dainty ankles decked with jewellery, painted toes peeping from a scandalous sandal.

Sarah was not stupid. She knew what fed her desire.

Because of her impediment, Sarah's feet were scrupulously clean. She pumiced, bathed, oiled, and perfumed them every evening. She kept her toenails perfectly trimmed and plucked the ugly black hairs that sometimes appeared on her big toe.

At her group, Sarah sat perched on the edge of her seat, her eyes wandering to the bronzed and slim ankle belonging to Cathy. And though she had no desire to sleep with a woman, she yearned to kiss and fondle the arched delicacy of Cathy's foot. Cathy turned to her.

'So Sarah,' she said, 'it's your go this week. What've you chosen?'

Sarah blushed and her hands fluttered uncertainly for a moment. She glanced at the manifesto hanging obliquely on the wall. 'I, uh,' she stammered, 'I mean ... my goal is to be more glamorous.' She stared down at her shoes.

'Good for you,' cried Carmen, clapping her hands.

'Yeah, that's great,' echoed Sally.

'About bloody time,' Suzy said. 'Wondered when you'd finally get round to it. You dress like my nana.' She leaned back into the soft folds of leather, her top gaping slightly to reveal a racy bra.

Suzy had been their most successful project. When she first came to the group she had weighed 90 kilograms. With the support and encouragement of the group she had managed to trim her succulent girth to a size ten. Whenever any of the girls were promoting their group they would crow about their success with Suzy. Sarah admired her greatly.

'You could start by getting rid of those ridiculous shoes,' Suzy said, pointing accusingly at the brogues.

'Remember, we're not here to be harsh,' Fran admonished as she turned her gaze to the manifesto.

'No, it's okay, really,' Sarah said, as the blush spread to her throat. 'That's really the crux of it. I realised this week. I'm never really authentic with anyone because I'm always conscious of hiding the secret, or worried they'll figure it out. And you know, I want to be authentic, but ... ah God, I'm uttering rubbish now ... I promised myself I wouldn't,' she muttered. Her hands slid down her right leg, past the long corduroy skirt, past the brown cotton socks, down to the neatly tied laces. Her fingers trembled as she released her foot from bondage. In a puritanical parody of a strip tease, she rolled the sock past her ankle, the arch and then the toes, finally revealing the secret.

Suzy stifled a gasp.

'You have very pretty feet, Sarah,' Fran said kindly.

'I would never have guessed,' from Barbara.

There was a general murmuring of reassurance from the group. Sarah searched their faces anxiously for any trace of mockery. But they were politely looking elsewhere. Except for Suzy whose twin lasers could have cauterised the object of scrutiny. Sarah followed Suzy's eyes. The sixth, a Napoleon of toes, was smaller and there-fore seemingly weaker than the others. However, it had waged war upon her field of flesh until it claimed dominion. And until now, Sarah, blonde and lithe, with eyelashes like a doe, had sub-mitted her body to the egomania of the sixth toe.

'I've decided to have it surgically removed,' she announced. 'Next week. I just felt that I had to say, you know?' The group whooped and cheered. Sarah laughed wildly, her lips stretched a little too thinly.

'Gee thanks, you guys are great.'

Her laughter eased and her hands escaped from her lap. They fluttered to her hair, her mouth, finally roosting beneath her chin.

'It will be so liberating, but you know ... it feels a little like I'm planning a murder ... I mean ...' her hands took flight, 'that little son of a bitch has been controlling my life.'

'I know!' Suzy smiled nastily. 'We'll give the little bastard a send off ... a funeral ... and get roaring drunk.'

*

The women stood in a ring, in the back corner of Sarah's garden. Shadows swooned across the foliage and a lone tree reached heavenward as if in suppliant devotion. Thirty or more tea-light candles glittered across the lawn, illuminating the women's faces from beneath. Sarah hobbled forward, her foot wrapped in layers of white cloth. She lowered a wooden tea-box into the hole.

'I don't mean to tread on your toes, Sarah ... well what's left, but I think a few words need to be said,' Suzy said, swaying slightly, with her champagne glass held aloft. 'After all, it is a grave matter.'

'Very funny,' Sarah said with a faint slur. Her hair was half its usual length, loose, and fell soft upon her neck and shoulders. Threads of it shone like captured sunlight in the glow of the candles.

'Thank you for coming this evening. It means a lot to me, you all being here. I don't think I could have taken this step without you.' She bit her lip, realising her unintended pun, her teeth pretty upon the fleshy red. 'It will sound silly I know, I could have done it years ago, but I think I needed that toe. I was using it as an excuse not to do the things I wanted to. And though it's only a toe, a small piece of flesh and bone, I feel immeasurably lighter. As though anything is now possible.'

The women hooted. Their faces appeared dangerously pagan.

'Fill up her glass!' Cathy shouted. 'She's way too ponderous for such an occasion.'

'No! It's only proper that the toe gets the send off it deserves,' Suzy said expansively. 'It's significant. We are here to bear witness as our friend lays a little piece of her past to rest. And with any luck see her bloom into the rose we know her to be.'

'For God's sake! Don't let Suzy have any more to drink,' Bianca said, grabbing the champagne from Suzy's clenched fist.

Sarah smiled thinly and trickled dirt into the hole.

*

Later that evening, after everyone had left, Sarah returned to the garden. Two candles waned and sputtered. It had been a mistake to have the women there, she realised. The whole evening had left her feeling slightly soiled. She stood still and silent in the darkness for more than an hour. Her eyes fixed upon the dark smudge of dirt at the edge of her lawn. After a while the candles expired and all that remained was a tepid glow from the moon. Finally, the hiss and screech of cats racing across the corrugated fences broke her daze. She returned to the house.

*

'Let's go shopping for a new wardrobe,' Suzy wheedled.

'I don't know,' Sarah replied.

'Come on. You said you wanted to be more glamorous. We'll buy you some lingerie, a dress and some fancy shoes. I've seen you ogling Cathy's strappy little numbers.'

'Oh, all right. I guess. But I don't have much money.'

'You're kidding, aren't you! I know you've got oodles. Old habits die hard,' she said, wagging a finger at Sarah. 'And that toe is going to keep its hold over you. Unless you find a way to break it. How do you think I got to be a size ten when I have to work in a patisserie?'

Sarah had often wondered. Especially after spying Suzy stuffing down three eclairs, one after the other, when she thought no one was watching.

*

That evening Sarah could not sleep. She kept thinking about the dress. She had bought it under pressure. It was melon coloured with a plunging neckline and a hem above the knee. Suzy had been mad about it, saying it made Sarah look like a goddess. Sarah had weakened under the seduction of compliments. But when she tried the dress on again at home, she cried. It made her feel like a slattern. Her breasts looked like ripe fruit, and the skin of her bare arms and neck seemed lewd.

She tossed and turned in her bed, as though this would shake off the vague and restless urge within her. The air in her room felt slick and oily upon her skin. It was unseasonably warm for March. She climbed out of bed, slipped into an old T-shirt and wandered out to the garden. At first her sly feet took her to the petunia bed. She leant down and crumbled a dead leaf between her fingers. Then she stroked a scarlet bloom that had folded in upon itself for the evening. It was her favourite texture, soft and velvety. Sighing, she stood up. Her foot itched where the toe had been removed and she began to stumble towards the patch on the lawn. But her will was stronger than her feet. She altered course and paced across the grass, kneeling in the dirt where her bulbs lay dormant. Scratching the moist earth she found a small tear-shaped freesia bulb. She loosened it from its bed and plopped it on the lawn. Her foot continued to itch but she resisted the urge to scratch. Sarah worked her fingers into a frenzy of excavation. Before long she had uncovered the whole bed of bulbs. For a long time she squatted there, wondering what to do with them. Eventually she replanted them; exactly where she had found them.

*

She returned the following evening. Gusts of wind whipped through the garden so that boughs and branches resembled women waving their arms in terror. Sarah's bare feet were numb with cold. She was punishing them for bringing her out again.

There was no moonlight. Heavy clouds pressed the sky thin and Sarah could almost feel their weight upon her. She faced the patch of soil. Her body knew exactly where the toe lay. Every now and then she wrung her hands.

Finally she turned and went to the little garden shed. The rusty door whined as it opened. She felt her way through the darkness, her hand skimming over cobwebs to the back corner where a lone implement stood. She grabbed it roughly by the neck, and dragged it back across the lawn. For a moment her foot hovered above the blade as she mustered her last shred of resistance. But this was not to be her Waterloo. She grunted as the blade punctured the soil. There was mild relief and a feeling of hollowness within her.

The blade scraped upon something, the wooden tea-box, Sarah realised instantly. The wind stilled and pale moonlight seeped through the clouds. She levered the shovel against the box. As it surfaced, moist clods crumbled from its top and sides. She brushed away the remaining dirt and lifted the lid. The toe looked small and innocent as it lay upon the bed of satin, already changing to a motley shade of black.

Sarah carried the box back inside, washed the toe in her bathroom sink, and patted it dry with some paper towels. In her pocket there was a glass vial on a chain. She drew it out and opened the lid. A sharp scent of methylated spirits made her cough. With the aid of tweezers she inserted the toe. After sealing the lid she gave the vial a little shake. Her toe bobbed up and down, finally settling somewhere near the bottom. She put it into its new resting place and flicked the bathroom light off.

In the bedroom she stood before the full-length mirror. The lingerie, the dress and the shoes were draped upon her bed. Sarah dressed. Her expression was serious and intent. Stepping back, she gazed in silent appraisal. The dress was just as provocative, the high heels accentuated the curve of her calf muscles, the eroticism of her ankles, and yet it now seemed okay. Her hunch had been right. The outfit had definitely been missing the right accessory. She fondled the glass vial that nestled in her cleavage.

River

Cassie Smith-Christmas

I
They paddle side by side,
those swans, bodies black
in the molten malachite,
red beaks striped with white –
Masai warriors picking
crumbs tossed by pig-tailed schoolgirls.

II
Four cygnets swim:
black beaks poking from
the white fluff of faces.
One parent hisses as I stoop
to photograph the babies
in their giant algae bathtub.

III
There are only three baby swans.
I do not know what happened
to the fourth.

IV
River walk at dusk:
A blue-breasted bird
needles his nose in the grass,
splicing dinner with his
two-pronged fork.

A rat, mistaken for a mink,
dives for supper and rises
empty-mouthed.

Leaves lie stuck to the surface of the water
like insects in a spider's web.

(In the middle, close to the bridge,
a fountain spouts to remind us that
somewhere
water does run,
but not on this earth).

A beach ball sunbathes
on a nest of algae two inches
from the shore. I imagine
the mother's voice as the child
carelessly tosses it into the river:
'Leave it, for the river will melt
your hands and then you'll die!'

Crested birds scatter as I, a human,
approach.
I do not blame them.

V
Returning:
A couple picks a stick
from a pile. With it, they
fish a bag from the river.

The swans group by the shore,
the autumn sun bright
on the babies' faces.

La Primavera

Christy Di Frances

1

Sal told her that the lilac bushes were coming into bloom, and she said, 'Are they really?' as if she didn't know already, as if she hadn't remembered those lilacs every single day.

'Oh, Laura,' Sal had told her, 'the lilacs have come into bloom, and I know how much you love them.'

She closed her eyes, trying not to think about the billowing bushes of muted purple so heavy with the scent of rain and May-time darkness. But she could see everything on that night before Sal's wedding.

Her mother's old-fashioned rosebush had gone deep pink beside the great stone archway. From her bedroom window, through many seasons, Laura had watched that rosebush grow tall from years of enduring such cold winters, illuminated by lanterns hanging above the porch.

Yes, at home it was night when those roses bloomed below the window. And tomorrow Sal would be married, but Laura would not wear pastel or carry white lilies down the aisle of the church.

'I wish that you were here,' Sal was telling her, across the thin phone line. 'I've been saying it all day. I keep on saying it to everyone – I wish that you were here.'

'I wish it,' Laura said, still remembering. The memories were themselves like roses, closing inward at the end of their time.

Later, after the line hung finally quiet, Laura hung up the phone. Inside her flat the air made no noise at all on that Sunday afternoon. It was not dark where she sat in falling shadows, not night in a land where autumn appeared in springtime.

When the silence became too thick, she took her key and went out, locking the door behind her.

2

Beneath the poplar trees, where the river ran, Laura could feel the autumn air. All along the riverbank the leaves were sifting down like blossoms turned gold from a crab-apple tree. Like snow and yet not like snow.

In the cool blue afternoon, she could not understand the sun-warm arc of river sparkles that touched the grass. She sat down on the bank beside a small cluster of poplar trees, drawing up her knees and hugging them tightly against herself.

On the river a model sailboat glided past, cutting the water's surface-silk film until all settled into calm. A moment later, two more tiny boats drifted by. They were there for the sailboat race, a competition for wooden boats, held on Sunday afternoons. Laura had heard it mentioned, but had forgotten.

She did not move. A woman wearing a grey business jacket over a navy blouse came and sat down beside her on a blanket. Laura smiled with effort, then looked quickly away towards the river to avoid conversation. The boats were beginning to line up – Tasars and Es and Herons, all in perfect miniature, their sails already filled with wind.

The race began and she tried to watch closely, to dismiss the entire world beyond boats painted yellow and bright blue. So, at first, she did not notice the old man wearing a straw hat, in his Oxford shirt and buttoned sweater, who came and sat nearby on the riverbank. When she finally did see him, she was struck by how fragile he looked, thin and worn as well-scrubbed cotton.

In one hand he held a fishing rod and from a black leather bag engraved 'S. Andrews', he took out tackle. Laura wondered what brought him there, to gaze all alone through thick lenses at the comings and goings of people in the park, at the still-sailing boats that had drawn a small crowd. But he was not alone – presently an elderly lady carrying a picnic basket came and sat beside him on the grass. Without saying a word she smiled at Laura from eyes that were really blue.

On her other side the grey-jacketed woman was asking, 'Perfect day for the race, isn't it?'

'Yes,' Laura replied, hoping that this would not be the start of a real conversation.

'I'd like to see the yellow one win,' the woman continued.

Laura nodded, saying, 'It's a lovely boat,' though secretly she admired the small green E with white sails.

Perhaps that is why, very close to the end of the race when the green E suddenly went under, Laura began to cry. She hadn't meant to, but she could not stop the tears that came in steady warm streams down her face. She felt them all looking at her: the grey-jacketed woman, the fisherman and his wife.

'I'm sorry,' she tried to apologise.

The woman in the business jacket handed her a handkerchief. 'No use crying about it, luv.'

And suddenly the fisherman's wife said, in a voice soft as river water, 'Let her cry.'

'Goodness,' the jacketed woman went on, 'it's only a *model* boat – it isn't even real.'

'No,' said the fisherman quietly, with a firm cast into the current beyond the reeds, 'it's more than that.'

The jacketed woman seemed irritated. 'Well, I guess I don't know.' She stood up rather quickly and shook bits of grass from her blanket before walking off toward the road. Laura tried to stop her tears with the handkerchief.

'Have some lemonade,' said the fisherman's wife, taking a thermos from her picnic basket and pouring golden-pale lemonade into a cup made of real glass instead of plastic. It was not at all the season for lemonade, but Laura took it to be polite and was surprised by its sweetness.

'Good?' asked the fisherman's wife. Laura nodded, noticing the necklace of seashells that she wore. All of the shells were translucent – cream coloured and edged in rich purple. They were perfectly shaped and uniform in size.

'Now,' said the fisherman, 'what is it?'

Laura turned her eyes back towards the river. She did not want to say the words to strangers.

'Tomorrow my friend will be married.'

'Your friend?'

'My sister . . . a friend like a sister. And I won't be there for her; I'll miss it all.'

The fisherman nodded and cast out the line a second time.

'Go on and cry,' said his wife, and she poured more lemonade into Laura's glass.

3

The afternoon light had begun to fade all around them. It shone quietly through the poplar branches that were going bare and reflected from the leaves, still green and glossy, of one tall eucalyptus with white skin smoother than any tree Laura had ever seen.

'You've never seen it before?' the fisherman's wife asked, as though she knew about Laura's thoughts.

Laura shook her head.

'It is beautiful though.'

'Yes.'

They were all silent, gazing up towards where the white eucalyptus rose to a rounded peak, joining with the poplar trees and evergreens in a wide circle that made the sky seemed domed. The dome was no longer only blue, but evening coloured with pink and orange and glowing violet.

The fisherman's wife, her hair seeming more gold than grey, leant toward Laura, smiling, 'Look into the water – the reflection is so real.' She held out her right arm towards the river, and Laura saw that she wore a cream-white bracelet of shells that matched her necklace.

Laura leant forward to look and something like a tear fell into the blue river, making the water like crystal. Astonished, she gazed into its clear depths, while all around the autumn leaves were falling, gold and white as wedding flowers.

The Sidhe's Song

William Brown

It is late afternoon but the sky's opaque surface isn't telling. Hector is only aware of the time because he's just left work at the site. The other boys drive home in beaten up pick-ups and old hatchbacks. The odd one peels away on a Harley or Ninja if the season is right. The foreman drives home in his new Ram. Hector walks. He doesn't mind it; it's convenient because he lives downtown just off the bus route. And the season is right for walking.

People pass him on the sidewalk, all intent on their own business. The crowd instinctively shifts around him as he marches against the flow: a boulder against the river. He is unaware of them. He would like to think it's because he doesn't care, but really it's because he cannot care. He has no choice right now. It's the same every time he takes this route. He is driven by a single purpose that is artificially significant to him. It is a desire that is not his own, but owns him nonetheless. It infuses his awareness, seizes it, and then directs it.

He turns down the alley, a familiar location for him. No pause to check over his shoulder, no loitering at the entrance until the street is clear. That is conspicuous. Hector moves along the alley confidently, as if just taking a short cut, when in fact it is his destination.

A gaunt figure huddles in an alcove against the chill wind. His clothes are filthy and his hair is unkempt, but that is just for appearances. He also reeks – that is for appearances, too: just a vagrant taking a break. Hector passes him, slows, and stops. He digs a few coins out of his jeans pocket and offers them to the figure.

'Cold day, Man. Here.'

'Fuck you.'

Hector sighs, digs in his jacket and pulls out a pack of cigs. He taps one loose. 'Smoke?'

'Now we're talking.'

Hector sits down on the low step and passes his lighter over. The Man lights up and admires the Chinese-style dragon on the side of the Zippo.

'This sterling?'

'Don't even think about it.'

'Just looking.' He passes it back. 'You steal it?'

Hector lights up. 'I won it in a poker game.'

'Right.' The Man shifts on the step. 'Shove over. You're crowding my office.'

'This is a fucking cramped office. I am over.'

'Whatever. You buying?'

'Yeah.' Hector draws again and holds the cigarette with his lips. He digs a roll out of his jacket and passes it under his arm. The Man pulls a loose brick out of the wall beside him with one hand. He rummages around inside. In a few moments he pulls out a small brown package. They exchange quickly with practised ease.

'That was fast, Man. How'd you know I was coming?'

'I'm "The Man". Customer service is my expertise.'

Hector flicks his cigarette away and gets up. 'Expertise? Stick to swearing, it suits you better.'

'Fuck you.'

'Take it easy, Man.'

'Later, Hell.'

'Don't call me that.'

'It's your name, ain't it?'

'Fuck you.'

*

The apartment he shares is lifeless when he gets home. It always is. The other two who live there are still in school. They wake up after Hector has already left for work, and get home after he passes out. Their lives are centred around campus, and they both have boyfriends. He only sees them on weekends if he's lucky. But they pay the rent, split the bills and leave the fridge to him, so they can spend as little time at home as they want. He doesn't mind. Or he says he doesn't.

That they are still in school and Hector isn't, doesn't mean they didn't do as well. They're on track. Hector dropped out. 'Taking a year off' was the story he gave to them and his family. Lots of students do it: work, travel, get your head straight. He isn't getting his head straight, though. And he isn't saving any money.

He doffs his steel-toes at the door and tosses his jacket over the armchair nearby. He shuffles over to the washroom to clean up. This is part of the ritual as well, and one of the last vestiges of Hector's control over his situation. There's always time to clean up a bit before getting fucked up, he insists to himself. He's not an addict, he chooses when and where, and wouldn't if he didn't want to.

As he passes the kitchen he catches a familiar sight out of the corner of his eye. Someone's been home, obviously. The counter is stacked with dirty dishes, and spilt juice has dried to a sticky residue. There's some on the floor, too, over a healthy base of crumbs.

'Goddamnit,' he swears to himself. How many times have I told them? Leave food around and you get bugs. The bastards don't need much of an invitation.

But he cleans the kitchen regardless. It doesn't take long. And when his room-mates leave a note later, thanking him with hearts dotting the 'i's, he won't mind. Or, he'll say he doesn't.

*

Later, with the ritual of returning home complete, Hector returns to the kitchen cleaned up, in sweats and a beater. He's carrying a small leather case from his room. It looks like a shaving kit. He takes a beer from the fridge, balancing it in his hand with the kit as he cracks it. The cap goes in an empty coffee can – something about raising money or materials for wheelchairs – and he moves into the den.

After digging the package out of his jacket he collapses in an old recliner with his entertainment arrayed around him. He shuts his eyes for a minute; this was a particularly hard day. Some of the boys at work are getting jealous of his size, he muses, or how fast he got this big. Or, maybe it's because I work as hard as three of those fuckwits combined. Never mind that; it's because he works so hard and so smart that he got in shape so quickly and can work harder, easier. It could be because the foreman has taken a liking to him and doesn't care what he does on break, just as long as he's in shape to work smart when he gets back. Whatever the reason, it's depressing that it has only been one season on site and the job's already going sour.

'Fuck 'em,' he says to himself as he leans forward for his beer.

He takes two swigs – he always takes two – then begins to set up his hit after taking off his leather bracer. Hector started wearing the bracers with his gloves to protect against flying chips of stone when using the sledges. When he first started the job they also helped his form when he got tired.

Now, they cover his tracks.

It was fortunate that he moved his hits down to his forearm after putting on his bulk because it was easier to find a vein there. His tracks were easily covered once they started to show. Call it dark luck – not good luck because it helps his habit, and not bad luck either, for the same reason.

Hell leans back in the recliner, sinking through the aged upholstery, into the waiting arms of his city's mercurial sky. Its plasma supports him and he hangs suspended in the scintillations of his hit. He rides its waves like he used to float in the surf at his grandparents' cottage, the salt content of the water keeping his slender form afloat. Its undulations are as familiar to him now as that coastline. He used to feel a thrill then, too, from doing some-thing wrong, or at least mischievous. His grandmother used to be particularly adamant that he not let himself float like that. What if he drifted away?

His name went bad as his life did, his nickname 'Hell' a constant reminder of his fall. 'Hector' to 'Heck' on a binge – it was a joke at the time, but it stuck. Then it turned to 'Hell' sometime later. He didn't really notice when, it was so gradual. At some point, each of his friends decided that Heck was too PC or something, so Hell took over.

*

Later, Hector rouses himself from his stupor into the waiting darkness of his apartment – not too much time later because the beer is still passable. Another couple of swigs and he sets about making dinner: cheap mini-pizzas in the microwave. It's not a healthy dinner, but it's about all he can manage in his state. The healthy food he saves for lunch and eats in bulk. It tastes better earlier in the day, anyway.

As he flicks on the kitchen light, there's a popping sound and the room remains dark.

'Oh, fuck,' he mutters.

By the light of the den he starts his dinner warming, then he heads to the hall closet where they keep the extra bulbs. The hall spins a bit, and he stumbles.

'That's . . . weird,' he manages.

He reaches over to flick the hall light switch. This time the popping noise makes him jump.

'What?' He stares up at the dead ceiling lamp. 'What the hell?'

He shuffles over to the hall closet in the gloom and reaches for the doorknob. The hall spins again and he steadies himself against the wall.

A few moments later he reaches again for the doorknob. A chill passes through his spine and he shivers. He pulls his hand back. Another chill passes through him. He can't help but look behind him. The apartment is motionless. He can hear the microwave still whirring away in the kitchen and the dull orange glow from its lamp spills pathetically into the hall.

He stares the other way into the gloom. The bedrooms are down there. His room-mates' doors are closed. There is nothing there.

'This is ridiculous!' he berates himself.

He reaches for the doorknob a third time. Again, the chill makes him shudder, and he stops short.

The microwave's alarm fires through his skull.

He stumbles back from the door and sits down hard. 'Goddammit. This is stupid.' He shakes his head, which is a bad idea, but the nausea passes shortly.

He opens the closet and retrieves the pack of bulbs without a problem. Then he shuffles back to the kitchen. He replaces the bulbs, not an intelligent thing to do when high, but it allows the pizzas time to cool so they don't burn his mouth when he devours them in front of the TV a few minutes later.

*

A stab of conscience hits him halfway through a reality-TV re-run. He remembers that his room-mates could walk in any minute. It's obviously not a shaving kit sitting on the coffee table with needles and a tourniquet inside. He lurches out of the recliner and packs his gear up quickly. He snatches up his empty beer as an after-thought. After rinsing it out in the kitchen sink, he chucks it back in the box with the other returns and heads to his room.

When he gets to his door, a dull thud behind him makes him jump again that night. Shit! Is someone home?

He calls out tentatively, 'Jill, is that you?' There is no answer, but he could swear the sound came from her room.

He approaches her door. 'Jill?'

Nothing.

He tries the doorknob. It's locked.

'Maybe it's the afterglow,' he mumbles to himself.

Two hours and a few more beers later he passes out in his room, empties rinsed and back in their case.

Fruit Flies at Work

Sim Ren

Every year it seemed more and more foreigners were crowding into the neighbourhood and Jimmy Bottle knew it was just a matter of time before something had to give.

When they first moved in with their two small boys in 1955, the Bottles were the only people within a five-mile radius of their bluestone cottage. Ten weeks later, a terribly large family from Orkney trudged down the same dirt tracks with their duffel bags and constructed their dwelling about a quarter of a mile away. Too close for comfort, hissed Clara Bottle behind her yellow curtains, peering through the window as if her ice-blue eyes could see that far, and her pink-shell ear could hear every thump and squeak made by Old Mac and his brood of 13 grubby younglings. Jimmy Bottle shrugged his skinny shoulders. What could he do? This was a free country and there were no laws restraining undesirable people setting up house near you. At least it was still bearable then, what with the rest of the settlers being Scottish, Irish, Welsh or English.

Then the unimaginable happened. Half a dozen Italian families moved in. Someone, it seemed, had decided to permit these settlers to relocate closer to the city instead of keeping them at Whyalla. These families had names too complicated to pronounce and impossible to remember, although the women were mostly Maria-something-or-other. *They* cannot be taught to speak English, *they* never get the sounds right, Clara Bottle liked to declare in the evenings when she brandished a dishcloth and scrubbed her one cooking pot, usually the remains of a pea or cabbage soup. Secretly though, Clara was more upset by the smells wafting into her spic-and-span home, brawny smells that came from boiling sauces and broiling meats in outdoor kitchens. Close the windows, she ordered her Bottle boys fiercely in the long days of summer. We don't want those smells coming in and spoiling the furniture. And Clara Bottle was glad when the peach trees they had planted around their property grew large enough to form some kind of a fence.

Hot on the heels of the Italians was a group of Greeks. But Clara Bottle couldn't tell the difference. Short, dark, loud and noisy, who could tell them apart? Jimmy Bottle thought he could recognise at least one of the men though. Galanopoulos, the fish-monger who had a stall at the East End market in town. This man sold them haddock. And Jimmy thought Galanopoulos' grecian nose was much smaller when compared to the roman beak. Oh shut up! was Clara Bottle's response to this ridiculous notion. One can't tell a wog just by the nose. Jimmy Bottle kept quiet then because he was the sort of chap who always did as he was told. But there was no doubt in his mind that it was after the Greeks that there was no stopping the explosion. Houses sprung up like mushrooms after a storm. Most of the scruffy eucalypts that dominated the landscape were hacked down and brick dwellings erected in their place.

Throughout this state of affairs, the Bottles kept a stiff upper lip. One foot in front of the other, one day at a time, until one fine afternoon when Jimmy was out in his yard watching galahs dive-bombing his trees, and the sun was beating down mercilessly on the 40 homes in the street: he heard a chugging sound and, glancing over the hedge, saw a man park his car in the driveway of the house next door and step out with what appeared to be his wife. The man spotted Jimmy Bottle's flushed red nose and tipped a hat at him. A fedora with a feather in it. Ah-lo! he said in a disconcerting accent. Goot dey for gardening, yah?

Jimmy fled back into his house. Clara, Clara, what's happened to the Hardys? Clara Bottle, making drop scones, eyed him with some disgust.

All week she had been talking about Sally Hardy and her man selling out and moving east to Sydney where her people were.

According to Lonnie the postie, the new people coming to this street would be a bunch of Schneiders.

Schneider? Jimmy Bottle clutched his plaid shirt where his heart was and staggered into a chair. Jerry, he groaned and reached both hands to pull his hair in an agitated manner. First the wogs, now the jerries; he had given six years of his youth fighting them in Europe and now they were at his doorstep. Hell and damnation!

Clara Bottle was strangely calm, almost as if she had resigned herself to sleeping with the enemy. She finished making her drop scones, walked over and poured some tea out for Jimmy and began to butter one of those scones with a smidgen of cream and jam.

A bite to eat, love? She offered the dainty morsel to her husband, who took it from her hand and carelessly eased the whole thing into his mouth. Clara Bottle smoothed his brow and said, There, there, we don't have to be afraid of the jerries; in this country, we outnumber them.

The presence of Herr Schneider made Jimmy Bottle a little bit more eccentric each day. He picked fruits off his trees surreptitiously, as if nicking from his own garden. By moonlight, he washed the bucket of bolts that was his Camira. In the mornings, with a large towel around his neck, he tiptoed across the lawn to pick up his mail and paper. He hunched and shuffled and developed a limp, and if you didn't know him you'd think he was at death's door. Come evening, when Clara sat in her easy chair watching her favourite soapie, he would play about with the volume knob, turning it down so low that Clara cried she couldn't follow the stories of Dave, Grace, John, Tom, Terry, Kitty, Harry and Rose.

Shush! Jimmy Bottle would place an ear to the wall and listen to see if he could hear Schneider breathing on the other side.

The following year, Jimmy Bottle was deliriously happy because someone came and offered to put up roller shutters in his windows for a small sum. Keep the cold out, the warmth in, the burglars away and the neighbours out of sight. Both he and Clara were disorientated by what they saw up and down the street. There were stone lions and gargoyles and naked little plaster boys weeing in fountains in the gardens of the Italian houses. The Greeks had painted their houses a glaring white, put in great pillars, and daubed their doors a bright blue. Some of these people had chopped down every native tree and shrub on their property, killed all the ivy, and terraced their lawns. The confounded Schneider turned out to be half Swiss and had a whopper of a cowbell for a door-knock.

But Jimmy's happiness was short-lived. A week after the shutters were installed, another exotic specimen sprung up in the neighbourhood. Black as midnight with two kids, a plump woman and a purple-duco wagon in tow.

What are they, negroes?

Clara Bottle ordered Jimmy out of the house to investigate. He had no choice but to walk over to Galanopoulos to ask. The fishmonger knew everything in the street. The new people were Bengalis from Calcutta: Mr and Mrs Majumder and their kids Rita and Ritu. Jimmy Bottle shuddered. How many Asiatics is the government going to let loose in this country? The answer was swift: the next morning a Chinese couple turned up and moved in next door to Galanopoulos.

Almost immediately, they dug up the rose bushes that had been planted there by the previous Italian family and erected what looked like a cairn, made up of crazy paving stones heaped in a corner. In front of this cairn-like edifice, they planted palm trees with red trunks. Clara Bottle was indignant. Killing roses and planting rocks and spooky palms! Jimmy Bottle suspected that the Chinese were up to feng shui, ancient geomancy to improve the luck of the home. This made Clara even more livid.

Feng shui my foot, they'd better not be jinxing us!

Then the Majumders started sending their kids up and down the street with platefuls of fried things. Clara refused to touch them or let anyone else have a try.

We don't know what's inside them, do we? Just like we don't really know what that mound of rocks opposite is supposed to do to the neighbourhood.

These remarks preyed on Jimmy Bottle's mind and he began

conducting surveillance on the Asiatics instead of Schneider. The whole summer, he spied on these two new families – following their women when they went to pick up groceries at the Bi-Lo down the road, to see what kind of foods and consumables they were buying; checking with the postie to see when they got mail from overseas; keeping a record of how often they switched on their porch lights; how frequently they had visitors over; how regularly the men wheeled out their rubbish bins as soon as they came home from work; what else they did or didn't plant in their gardens.

While this activity soothed Jimmy Bottle and gave him a sense of security, his daily reports to Clara Bottle on the goings-on of the Bengalis and the Chinese made her more nervous than ever, and she began to have nightmares when she slept. Every night, she saw fruit flies alighting on her beloved peaches. The golden-pink fruit became mottled and grey as these insects invaded tree after tree in her garden. Clara Bottle saw this as a sign and told Jimmy so.

Things are going to get worse; the fruit flies will take every peach we have in this garden.

Jimmy Bottle, having become fuzzy and doddery since his pre-occupation with first Schneider and now the Asiatics, assured Clara he would ring up Quarantine and get some form of pest control.

Summer faded away and as the days grew shorter and the skies gloomier, Clara Bottle became more despondent. Perhaps they should sell their house and move to another suburb? After all, now that the Bottle boys were grown up and gone away, the house was too big for two oldies like themselves.

A unit by the sea would be lovely, wouldn't it?

Jimmy Bottle thought about it a bit and decided, once again, that the missus was right. As soon as spring came, he'd sell.

That very evening, for the strangest reason, it began to storm. Clara, watching *Better Homes and Gardens,* and Jimmy, napping on the couch, were at first oblivious to the storm. Both were so relieved at the prospect of leaving the neighbourhood, they couldn't care if the roof fell on their heads. But the storm grew worse and a gale force wind tore through the street at several hundred kilometres an hour. This wind ripped off Jimmy Bottle's garage roof and knocked down the sole eucalypt in his front yard. The tree crashed into a stobey pole and plunged the entire street into darkness. Clara screamed and jerked out of her chair.

Jimmy, get up!

Jimmy had heard the loud gurgle and choking of their fridge just before it died but thought it was Dr Harry with an old Saint Bernard. Clara walked over and pinched his arm. Jimmy opened his eyes.

Blast! A blackout.

He put on his robe and slowly felt his way around the room until he found the torch on the hallway table. Thus armed, he opened the front door and went out.

The wind that wreaked the havoc had disappeared, leaving behind a light drizzle. Jimmy shuffled out to the street where a small knot of people were standing, looking at the fallen eucalypt and the demolished stobey pole. What is to be done? The Chinese man seemed mesmerised by the exposed live wires dancing up and down on the Bengali family's lawn. Both the Chinese man and his wife were in their flannel pyjamas and cotton slippers and shivering in the rain. Nitwits, thought Jimmy Bottle.

Anybody hurt? he asked, not looking at Schneider and Galanopoulos who were shaking their heads and loudly proclaiming what hazards big trees could be in a residential area like this. Vair-ry close call, coulda struck da house, made pretty mess. Galanopoulos seemed to be enjoying frightening everybody.

Inside the house, Clara Bottle wrung her hands and, as the seconds ticked away, decided a cuppa was just the thing to calm her down. Doggedly, she made her way to the kitchen and put water on the gas stove to boil. Then, as she turned to pick up a cup, her hand touched the tea kitty, sweeping it to the floor. Tiny pieces of ceramic peppered her ankles. No, I shan't panic. Clara steeled herself and bent down to pick up the shards of the broken kitty. The next thing she knew, she was on the floor with her right leg in a funny angle to her hip. She stared at herself. What was going on? She touched her hip but there was no pain. In fact, she had no feeling at all. By the time Jimmy came back inside, Clara Bottle had lost consciousness.

*

Two weeks passed. Clara Bottle was declared ready to go home. The moment Jimmy turned up at the hospital, she knew something was wrong. Jimmy looked guilty and Galanopoulos was standing by his side, smirking like a siamese cat.

Time to go home, dear. Sam here drove me. You know how I can't see very well when it rains.

Clara looked at Galanopoulos and wondered since when he had become a Sam.

She refused to talk in the car and sat staring out the window. Her disquiet grew when they pulled up at her house. The air was different. She wished she could get out from her wheelchair and walk into the house as she had always done. The indignity of being trundled down her own driveway by a rascally fishmonger was almost enough to make her scream.

The front door swung open even before they reached it.

Hello, Mrs Bottle, welcome home.

Clara Bottle gaped at the Bengali woman standing in her doorway, wearing her apron, holding her favourite cooking spoon, the one with a tulip-shaped handle.

An omelette, in case you're hungry, said this usurper, offering a plate with her other free hand. Clara sniffed garlic and backed away. She tried to turn and look at Jimmy, but he wouldn't give her his eye.

You just rest and leave everything to us, boomed Mrs Majumder, walking away with the odorous omelette.

Us? Almost as if she were a mind reader, Mrs Majumder answered: I must get back and start dinner in my own house. Mrs Hew will come in shortly.

Mrs Hew? What Mrs Hew? Clara panicked and stared at her lounge room. Everything was in its place, yet something was amiss. Galanopoulos and the Bengali woman left and Jimmy scuttled off somewhere, leaving Clara alone and bewildered.

Jimmy! Jimmy! But he was out of earshot. Clara Bottle, with great effort, wheeled herself to her bedroom. She struggled out of her cardigan and looked around for a hanger. There was none in the usual basket by the side of her bed, so she moved towards the wardrobe. Blow! How was she to reach those hangers?

Jimmy! Jimmy! An anger she hadn't felt for a long time burned at her throat.

Sorry I was late, Mrs Bottle. Clara jerked at the sound of the unfamiliar voice. What do you need, Mrs Bottle? Let me get it.

Clara was frightened. Who are you? What are you doing in my house?

The stranger became flustered and dismayed. Oh, so sorry, so sorry. You don't remember? I, Mrs Hew, from house across the road.

I want Mr Bottle. Where is Mr Bottle?

Oh, my husband with him, gone to shops. Buy some things for you.

Clara Bottle was angry enough to spit bullets. She looked around her room. Neat as a pin, just as she had always kept it.

I don't need anything, she glared at the youngish Chinese woman. Just leave me alone. I want rest, understand, rest!

Mrs Hew got the message and left, closing the door softly behind her. Clara touched the lilac bedspread of her mattress. Her fingers were trembling so much she could hardly believe they were a part of her wheelchair-bound body. What's happening in this house? Now, the pain she was supposed to have felt when she broke her hip came surging through her body all at once. She put out one hand to steady herself for the transition between her chair and her bed but the hand slipped and her knees buckled. She had forgotten to lock the wheels and now the chair rolled back. Clara tried to reach for something but grasped air and fell face down onto the floor, her two feet kicking the wheelchair and sending it crashing into the bedroom door.

The door flew open. Tears streamed down Clara Bottle's face as she felt two wiry arms pick her off the carpet and turn her body around.

Don't cry, Mrs Bottle, please.

The Chinese woman placed her arms around Clara's neck. Clara had no choice but to cling on like a rag doll. After a few huffs and puffs, the woman succeeded in manoeuvring her onto the bed. Mrs Hew breathed loudly and pushed a stray lock of hair out of her eyes. Clara saw that she was only about 25.

Without knowing how, Clara fell asleep. And she did not know how long she slept. But when she opened her eyes, she spied Jimmy peering at her from the bedroom door.

Oh Jimmy, what's happening!

She put out her arms and old Jimmy shambled over. He sat on the edge of the bed and put his head on Clara's chest. His words came out in a rush.

Sorry love, couldn't cope, all alone, never learnt to cook, and all that cleaning.

Clara Bottle stroked his head. Poor darling.

Jimmy sighed, a long tired sigh, and eased into bed beside her. He fell asleep with her hand still on his brow.

Two hours later, Clara awoke a second time, startled by a loud humming. At first she suspected the young Mrs Hew was vacuuming the house. But then she realised the sound was coming from above her head. She shook Jimmy. He opened a bleary eye.

Time for tea already?

No, Jimmy. That sound. Listen. What is that?

That's a vacuum cleaner, love. Jimmy dropped back into his pillow.

Yes, but coming overhead? Hear that?

Jimmy took so long to respond that Clara thought he might have fallen asleep again. He turned on his elbow to gaze at her.

That's Schneider, he said at last, grinning.

Schneider?

Yes.

The jerry, Schneider?

Yes, dear.

But what's he doing?

He's vacuuming the roof. Lots of leaves and broken twigs from the storm. Gutters are all clogged.

But vacuuming the roof? What next!

Jimmy shifted slightly. Should he or should he not tell her about Mrs Vitalli who would be coming in tomorrow to help with the laundry?

Love, he started, but she put a hand on his mouth. Jimmy, didn't I warn you about the fruit flies?

Yes, love.

What did I say about those fruit flies?

You said they'd be eating up our peaches.

That's right.

We're too old to fight the fruit flies. Clara mumbled, drifting off again.

Yes, love, too old.

Jimmy looked at the woman quietly snoring beside him and wondered how the both of them had suddenly grown so old. He lifted Clara's palm to his lips and kissed it.

Don't worry, love, I'll always protect you.

The humming overhead was a soothing buzz now. Schneider must be vacuuming further up the back of the roof. Jimmy Bottle closed his eyes and a curious thought came to him.

Damn the peaches, tomorrow he'd see a man about planting olives.

Frozen

Anna Solding

Across the expanse that is the frozen dam, jellybean children sail
effortlessly, making a mockery of her wobbly knees and static feet.
Bodil breathes in deeply, lets the cool air fill not just her lungs but
her entire being, leaving a soft, frosty coating on her nerves.

She knows she can do it. She can do anything she really sets out
to accomplish. Not that ice-skating even remotely resembles the
kind of things she would normally try but she knows she can do it.
Her husband Ben and six-year-old son Andy wave from the far end
before pushing off back towards her. The ice is thick and uneven,
covered in a layer of the snow-like shavings created by skaters who
practise quick and cool turns. There aren't many of those young
hoons at the moment, rather the opposite; all she can see are
families linking chains or chasing each other. She should be a
link in her family's chain, but she has lost all contact with her
squashed feet, encapsulated in layers of wool and hard plastic,
and they won't obey.

'Mummy, come on! Don't you want to skate with us?'

Bodil looks at her son and sees her father's enthusiasm and
curiosity in deep-blue eyes resembling her own. He is a perfect
mix. Sometimes she thinks he is too good to be true.

'I'm trying. I think I might have forgotten how to do it.'

Andy looks at her, astonished.

'But Mum, it's like riding a bike. Once you know how to do it,
you never forget.'

She smiles at her own words that jump like little frogs out of his
toothless mouth.

'Maybe I never knew to begin with . . .'

The child slides next to her and slowly pushes off with his left foot, then his right, then turns around, triumphant.

'Look at me, Mum. If I can do it, you can.'

She exchanges a loving glance with Ben as he offers her his hand, hidden deep inside a woollen glove that she knitted in one of her weaker moments. The gloves resemble misshapen socks more than anything, but he continues to wear them, either out of love for her or because he likes the way that they make her slightly flustered from embarrassment and just a little pride.

'Now, let's try this slowly. Bend your knees. Slowly. Balance. One foot at a time. That's it! You're doing it.'

Considering he learned to ice-skate inside an artificial mountain in the southern hemisphere, he isn't a bad teacher. With triumph in sight, she doesn't notice the little mulatto girl with a shock of white hair. She comes out of left field, crossing her path at speeds she has never even dreamed of, and before she has time to say 'shoo baloo' she is lying in a heap on the ice, laughing herself silly. Andy falls on top of her and cries with laughter.

'Mum, you looked sooooooo funny!'

When did she start letting go? Since when is it fine, or even desirable, for her child to laugh at her failures? She can't remember, but she is happy that it is so. She is the luckiest woman in the world.

The sun skates quickly across the yellow sky. When Ben asks if she'd like to pause for *fika* she realises that it has been two hours since they arrived and her stomach is screaming for coffee and scrolls. Without falling a single time she skates across to the far side, holding Andy's steady little hand in hers. The backpack is where they left it and she unpacks foam seats, mugs and buns. Andy ends up with a sugary face and a chocolate moustache.

Bodil's back aches. A dull, strangely soothing pain. No more ice-skating for her today, she decides. She has done more than enough.

'Yummy scrolls, Dad.'

She agrees. 'Yes, they're superb, my love.' She leans over to kiss Ben.

Andy turns away, making a face. 'Do you have to do that? Yuk!'

Bodil and Ben laugh and try to kiss him, too, but he makes himself slippery and shoots off onto the ice.

'Be careful, Andy. I'll be with you in a minute,' Ben shouts after him in English.

As Bodil leans back on the slope, the pain in her back spreads to her stomach. Like an anaconda that has decided to wind its body around hers and then squeeze, the pain has no intentions of letting go. She closes her eyes and breathes deeply. Her period pains aren't usually this strong.

'What is it, Bodil?'

'Nothing,' she replies.

He keeps looking at her, quizzically.

'My back hurts. Probably just the ice-skating. Or maybe my period . . . it isn't as regular as it used to be.'

He packs the thermos and the mugs without taking his eyes off Andy. Finally, he turns down to her with pinched cheeks and a furrowed brow. 'Let's go home, then. Looks like you need to lie down.'

'No, no. I'm fine. I'll just stay here and watch the two of you.'

'Are you sure?'

Without warning the anaconda constricts around her lower abdomen and her head falls forward between her legs. She breathes quickly, clenching her teeth. This is like childbirth. But how could she be in labour when she isn't pregnant? Hasn't been pregnant since they had Andy. They tried to again for years, but it just never happened. She is too old. The ravenous hunger, the vomiting, the fatigue – there were none of the signs that indicate pregnancy. Her medical brain keeps ticking behind a screen of pain. Why now?

From very far away she hears Ben's voice trying to reach her, but she has no strength to look up. Must breathe. She feels his hand on her shoulders and sweat running down her forehead. If only she could stand up, the pain would pause before the next stab. Suddenly, she is hotter than she has ever been before. Flames are gushing from every pore of her body, a flood of lava between her legs.

'Bodil. Please, Bodil, speak to me.'

There is a pause. Then she hears him scream to Andy not to look, to go around the other side to wait, and she hears Ben whisper to God to make everything all right, something she's never heard him say before, and she opens her eyes and all she can see is red and she knows this is how it feels to be dying.

'Can we have an ambulance to Pildammsparken. The ice-skating rink. Now! I'm a doctor.' Ben's Swedish doesn't flow well when he is stressed.

His hands are shaking when he puts the mobile phone back into his pocket. The green gloves are on the ground next to the widening spread of red snow. How ugly those gloves are. If she survives this she'll knit a new pair, brown to match his eyes. She wants to laugh, but all that comes out is a whimper. The heat is eating her up from the inside. She is burning to death.

'Don't worry, Andy. Mummy will be fine. We just need to get her to hospital as soon as we can.' Ben doesn't quite sound like he believes his own words.

Bodil hears her son's silence.

Did she wish for too much? Hadn't she given up hope of ever giving him a brother or sister? A desperate attempt from a body no longer suited for a second bout of the strenuous work she never expected to do once? She wasn't supposed to have children at all. Yet Andy appeared like a gift. But this little lump of cells pushing out of her will never be a baby.

As the blood escapes her body, so does the heat. Her hands start shaking and she feels her face turn into a mask of ice. Every breath of air fills her lungs with crystal compressing into glaciers.

'Bodil, please say something.' Ben speaks in English, now. His smooth Australian melts some of the ice. 'Speak to me. You need to stay awake.'

A small crowd has gathered a few metres away, she hears them mumbling. Her head is light and cold. The pain has subsided, exists only as a memory of life that could have been. She looks up and searches for Andy's face behind Ben's broad shoulders. Ben's eyes are cloudy but he manages a smile. Her eyes get caught in their love.

'I want to go to work,' she croaks.

He shakes his head in amazement. She is losing blood but not her quirky sense of humour.

'Don't worry, they are on their way. Once you are there you can work as much overtime as you like. But you need to get there first.'

Her nails are leaving imprints on the back of his hand. Again, she looks for Andy, a shadow of his dad. Without letting go of Ben's hand, she reaches out for her son. She breathes the sweet smell of his skin and she knows she is the luckiest woman in the world.

Waiting Room

Emilie Field

No need to say tomorrow –
no sense in sending for new stacks
of magazines to blur the hours:
it will not be long.
Before your chairs become hostile
and smiles too long sustained begin to crack,
your night watch will be aborted,
and you can all turn back.
Yet waken faith for its last fight
lest it bend and bleed this hour;
rest not hope on fading days –
she knows she only has this night.
Even now the flame that lights her eyes
wavers in the winds of death:
some have had their turn already –
she'll be called in next.

Home Ground

Carol Lefevre

I begin to miss Tom the instant I lose sight of him waving from the observation deck. From Heathrow to Hong Kong, the image of his raised arm waving a folded newspaper replays in my head, as I list the arguments that have propelled me onto this plane. After two decades of yearning, I have given in to the long weariness of home-sickness. These are the sacred words: jacaranda, oleander, frangipani, sarsaparilla. I recite them miserably but am not comforted.

Flying over Australia in the early hours of the morning, the ancient and ravishing beauty of the landscape is gradually revealed by the rising sun. I rest my eyes upon luminous ridges of red sand. Shadows of trees stretch slender fingers, softening the contours of a landscape that will be harsh by midday.

Home. I trace the swirling lines and loops of dried up riverbeds, finding not a straight line anywhere, until the man-made scratches of a road appear. The dots of trees give the flat surface, with its snaking lines, the look of an Aboriginal painting, as if they have always known this terrain from 35,000 feet. To fly for hours over the solid emptiness of Australia is a source of intense comfort, probably inexplicable to Europeans bred on handkerchief-sized kingdoms.

Gina sleeps beside me, her dark head drooping. I've shredded the past, I think, shuddering at the pain of the final days, of Tom's face as I crumpled paper to pack china into crates. Shaking, leaking doubt from every pore, I had climbed onto the plane, only buoyed up by Gina's excitement. Gina still has not grasped the full flavour of our going. At 13, her thoughts are of surfing and swimming and sideways looks at boys.

*

And so at last I have returned to the thick-walled stone villa I often inhabited as a child. The polished floors are cool and clean underfoot as I drift, aimless as a sleepwalker, through the dim familiar rooms, protected from the clamour of heat and light by heavy curtains. Although I have longed to soak in strong light, I am grateful for these shaded rooms, for we have arrived in the middle of a heatwave. Each night the house creaks and groans in sympathy as I lie in the stuffy darkness, mourning Tom. Through a stretch of scorching days it shields us like a living skin, until the cool change blows in from the sea with a swell of net at the open windows. Then rain sings on the tin roof and the wind roaring in the chimneys and rattling the ancient sash windows breaks the silence, in which I sit stricken with loneliness. Tom and I have been parted before, but always with a date for a reunion.

Still, there is solace in inhabiting a long-familiar space and I feel suddenly as if in all my restless life I have failed to find a pattern that matches this one exactly. Probably this stone house, with its cooing wood pigeons, its dust-furred cellar where geckos scuttle, has set my concepts of space and light for all time. Sadly, it is no longer mine. I abandoned it thoughtlessly, years ago. My mother's touch is indelibly impressed on every room and my grandmother lingers too. In the corners of the wardrobe, in the empty dressing-table drawers, I press a fingertip and gather ancient particles of loose face powder, fine dust left over from the lives of the women who inhabited this house before me. I would be grateful now for their company and advice, but in the brown speckled glass I meet only my own troubled gaze.

Our two suitcases, spilling clutter, have burst upon the orderly rooms like a pair of masked intruders. For all its familiarity, I am a stranger here and Gina, too, once the first ecstasy of running from the house to the sea is over, has discovered that she is a camper. From the corner of my eye I register the discontented thrust of her chin towards a childish alphabet hanging above her bed and the wooden horse belonging to some grown-up cousin that straddles the empty fireplace in her bedroom.

I wait for Tom to ring.

'I want to swim.' Gina is fretful, with a whine hatching at the back of her nose.

'Just wait for the phone and then if it's not too dark we'll go together,' I plead, but her eyes flash and suddenly Gina is beyond reach. Exhaustion and the kaleidoscope of changes have catapulted her into that no-man's-land where 13-year-old girls, all jutting chins, elbows, and irrational impulses, run the gauntlet of parental displeasure.

'I want to go.'

'You can't. Not right now.'

'You can't stop me!' Gina slams the front door and runs into the street. I know it to be futile but rage propels me after her. 'Come back now! You hear me?'

Gina's bare feet slap the pavement as she marches stiff-legged towards the sea. She's wearing bathers and the straps crossing her back have slipped, revealing two crescents of paler skin. In the 24 hours since our arrival, Gina's olive complexion has responded to the sun.

I lunge forward and catch her arm.

'Leave me alone!'

Gina pulls back hard and pushes her chin forward into the space between us. Still I cling to her. I even manage to drag her a few inches in the direction of the house before the strength, the defiance oozing from her, defeats me.

My panic and shame rise like floodwaters as Gina flicks her hair over her shoulders and stalks away towards the sea.

*

In the bedroom, licking tears from my lips, I dial the long series of numbers that will connect me with Tom in England. As I listen to his telephone ring, the front door clicks softly. Gina has returned.

'Give it time, Lily, you've only just arrived,' says Tom.

Choking on tears, I thrust the telephone at my daughter.

'Daddy, I want to come home,' she cries, as I wander out into the darkened garden.

Tom's voice was as warm and steady as always. I lift my face to

144

the canopy of leaves rustling overhead. I have left my husband for a jacaranda tree in flower.

*

At the station where, as a schoolgirl, I waited sitting on a brown Globite school-case, I buy a ticket from the swarthy Italian in the kiosk. Enthroned in his little shed, he is like a king in his castle, having turned his ticket booth into a tiny cell of his own home, split off and grafted onto the concrete slab of a suburban railway platform.

Arias pour from the tape player, an electric fan keeps the heat at bay, the aroma of freshly percolated coffee drifts from the tiny kitchen out back where he fixes lunch. He has made the kiosk so homely that his customers linger to chat, until the hoot of the train sends them scurrying.

Hairy forearms reach under the counter for the ticket.

''S a dollar sixty.' His accent is thicker than his waistline and his waistline is that of a man whose wife knows the way to his heart. He's a lucky man.

From the train I gaze with dismay upon rows of utilitarian houses, broad bands of traffic, bus shelters disfigured with the livid acne of graffiti. I remember with a pang the house I have recently abandoned, its winding stair, cast-iron fireplaces and tall windows with folding shutters. It belongs to someone else now. I mustn't think of it. What would have happened if Tom and I had never met? I would have come home years ago. But to what? Would I be pouring over plans for one of these dull brick houses on some suburban allotment, plotting to cover the space between plants in the landscaped front yard with pebbles or bark chips? I used to dream of a garden with orange and lemon trees, peaches, apricots, old-fashioned roses and topiary birds in faded terracotta pots.

In the side streets of the city I search out its espresso heart. At the Café Buongiorno, couples crowd the outside tables, smoking, sipping strong black coffee from tiny cups. Inside, it could be any-where in Italy, with the hissing Gaggia, the stacks of creamy espresso cups, the tubs of gelati and the roar of conversations at full throttle. In a sad trance, I listen to the rise and fall of my own language. Words I have not heard in years leap out, recovered in a split second with all their shades of meaning intact. It's a convivial atmosphere and in the espresso desert of the north of England there is hardly one such place. Perhaps, I think wishfully, I might live like a migratory bird, departing at the end of each cool northern summer to beat my way south.

*

In the mornings, while the pavements rest in the shade of the houses, I walk, soaking in gardens, casting greedy eyes over neat lawns, manicured shrubs, rows of white standard roses and the deep verandahs of Federation villas. In back lanes I discover the wild gardens where arms of frilly hibiscus and vines lunge over ramshackle fences, where rosy pomegranates dangle beside passion-fruit and laden quince trees. I pause to rub and sniff, crushing leaves to breathe the antiseptic scent of tea-tree, the pungent sap of the slender leaves of the pepper tree. Here, frothing over brush fences, are plants I had forgotten: lantana, plumbago, tacoma, bottle-brush, the dazzling bird-like strelitzia and dreamy blue heads of agapanthus, which conjure the image of my mother, Ginny, teacup in hand, on an early morning tour of the garden.

'Such agapanthus this year!'

For years I imagined these plants must secretly belong to the animal kingdom: hippopotamus, rhinoceros, agapanthus.

The hiss of sprinklers was the early morning and twilight music of childhood and I listen to it now with sad delight as I wait for a sign.

*

In the late afternoon, Gina and I walk the length of the esplanade where new houses fight for elbow room; it was all sand hills when I was a child. I shade my eyes and search the cliff at the end of the bay where my aunt's old house perches, embedded in vines and trees, above the dry gullies we once roamed as cowboys and indians. These gullies are crammed now with gaunt structures of glass and steel. A rare piece of vacant land drips pigface, cactus, and waving stalks of bunny tails.

'It used to be like this all over,' I say, but Gina has no interest in the past.

A tiny dog materialises at our feet, a poodle, wagging its stump of tail and panting in the heat.

'Where did you come from?' I bend to pat its curly head.

A girl jogs past on the other side of the road. 'Not mine,' she shouts and keeps on running.

Gina stoops to pick up the dog. 'He hasn't got a collar.'

In the creature's soft bewildered eyes I meet the trusting gaze of my own dog, Cosy, left along with Tom in England and no doubt probing the chilly air for clues to the vexing problem of our absence. Cosy's little footpads are tough from running on the shingle beach in all weathers. For weeks now she will have run and run, chasing seabirds, breasting sudden swells of icy saltwater and looking back to find only the lone figure of Tom leaning into the wind on the few yards of frozen sand at the water's edge. In the solid heat of a summer afternoon I shiver at the image of their solitary shapes pressed beneath the marble slab of winter sky.

Gina cradles the stray dog with the same enslaved expression she wore when she came home from the boating lake carrying a rescued duckling. My response now is the same.

'Gina, we can't keep it.'

'Well, we can't just let him get run over!' Gina's voice is spangled with overtones: the everyday teenage irritation she feels towards me and the polarised opinions she holds about liking where she is and yet feeling uprooted.

Behind us, a woman in baseball cap and trainers ushers a white standard poodle onto the pavement. She turns with a relieved smile.

'I've been terribly worried about this little fellow. I saw him from my window, darting among the traffic.'

'It's not ours,' I say, registering a creeping desperation in my voice.

'He hasn't got a collar,' Gina still hugs the panting dog protectively.

'He looks very well cared for.' The woman is a neat greying blonde who has powdered her nose with care before stepping out on her walk. 'He must have escaped.'

'We can't take it,' I say, 'we've only just arrived.'

'Oh!'

'He needs a drink,' Gina says, eyeing the dog anxiously.

I close my eyes against the enamelled glare and the sight of my daughter nursing the stray dog so tenderly.

'Keep an eye on Angeline and I'll find a lead and collar.' The woman pronounces her dog's name 'On-geline' and presses the lead into my hand. Angeline swivels plaintive eyes after her departing mistress. On the other side of the road, two women pass, leading a miniature poodle.

I wave. 'Do you know who owns this little one?' I cry, eager to divert Gina to the search for its rightful owner. The women cross over and Angeline lunges forward.

'BJ, behave!'

We are surrounded by white poodles of every size.

'There's a house further along where a little white dog sits in the window,' says BJ's owner. 'This looks like the dog.'

'Someone will be heartbroken,' says her companion.

I look at Gina's flushed face.

Angeline's mistress returns. 'I've found a lead but I had a little trouble with the collar.'

Angeline swoons towards the woman as she produces a piece of twine and ties it round the little dog's neck. He licks her hand in gratitude as she clips on a lead.

Gina sets him down on the footpath and BJ leans forward to nuzzle.

'I'll take him along and see if anyone's in,' says BJ's owner, and I sag with relief as Gina relinquishes the little dog to the two women.

*

'Tom, I want to come back.'

'Are you sure?' Somehow my husband keeps his grip on sanity, even in extreme circumstances.

'You sound as if you don't care.'

'I miss you, but I don't want you to be miserable and –'

'I'm so lonely without you. It's taken all the pleasure out of being here.'

'How's Gina?'

'Oh, having a great time.'

'Well, maybe –'

'It's not enough. I know that now.'

At the other end of the telephone, Tom sighs. Is it relief? Exasperation? Without seeing his face, I can't tell. In my mind he is far away, sealed behind glass, waving the folded newspaper from the observation lounge at the airport. Every time he raises his arm I want to scream.

*

'I won't go back! You can't make me,' Gina is gearing up for a struggle.

'But you told Dad you wanted to go home –'

'I meant I wanted to *see* him, I didn't mean I wanted to go back! I'm happy here, I'm saving up for a really good bodyboard from the surf shop.'

Gina shakes her hair as if that settles the matter. I stare helplessly at my daughter, this child to whom I have longed to hand over my own sun-soaked childhood. At what expense have I wrenched back the past? Now Gina, grasping it firmly, has made it her own.

*

In the hammock, swinging in blue shade, I make a careful list: souvenir de la malmaison (in memory of Empress Josephine, another exile); the incense rose; the beautiful damasks, hebe's lip (creamy white, tipped with red), and quatre saisons (oldest of the repeat flowerers). I suck the pencil and close my eyes. The ropes of the hammock creak. I lie back, gazing up beyond the leaves and the greenish purple globes of the ripening figs to the jigsaw pieces of blue sky. This is a dream list of roses for a garden I could, if I returned to England, dig and plant, manure, prune and nurture as carefully as I have nurtured the memory of childhood.

I take out the letter I have written to Tom. Strange to think that in a week this same envelope will drop into a letterbox on the other side of the world, that Tom will place his hand where mine is now and gaze at the rolling stems and loops of my writing. I fold the list, slide it in beside the letter and seal the flap, holding it for a moment against my dry lips.

Cradled by the hammock, suspended in warm air, my eyes close as I make the gradual drift into that dreamy state which is neither sleeping nor waking but is more restful than either. In this drowsy stillness, if I am lucky, I will find the entrance to that long thin country on the edge of sleep, which is the only neutral territory I can possess, my only true home ground.

*

My sister spots the picture in the card rack at Dymocks.

'This is you, Lily,' she says.

I lean over her shoulder and look. It is a reproduction of *The Drover's Wife* by Drysdale, monumental, solitary, her back turned to the landscape where a tiny covered wagon waits. In a peculiar way, it does look like me.

I pay for the card and stow it in my bag. As ever, when preparing to leave, I snatch at things I can take with me, as if with planning and careful packing I could fit the whole of Australia into my suitcase.

After lunch we kiss goodbye and I step out into the honeyed afternoon light. High up the sky is an endless blue-gauze freeway streaming away in all directions. Above my head birds flutter in the leaves, while in my grandmother's garden, ripe figs drop sound-lessly into the long grass.

Sickness Unto Death

Emmett Stinson

No, okay, but wait, because the thing is you have to understand this – it were Jack caught the fever first where we'd come directly to my parents' old place further out in the country, right after, just a few years before, and tried to go on with the business of living best we could. It were still shortly after the event, but before we knowed about the plague, though we damn sure enough found out about it, but it was that goddamned Rider come out a nowhere did the whole damn thing anyways, and so still there weren't no electricity nowhere no more. That stopped right after the event, but you still saw cars, and you could get gas if you knew who to ask and what to trade – not like now – so we brought him upstairs to the room on the second floor that had been the guest room when I was growing up, just next to a tree and least directly in the midday sun, so it stayed coolest. Jack was weak and sweaty but that was all so far. We hoped for the best, and Emile said we should've never let that Rider near here. I agreed but didn't nod because we couldn't be sure it was anything but a fever, not yet. The Rider was covered head to toe in sores and had already stopped breathing during the night, but all them red blotches on his body looked a constellation of lesions like all of the sins that he committed in his entire life rose up through his body and come out his skin.

He had appeared three days ago – more people were using horses now, going back to the old ways. He was pale, skinny. His hat sat awkwardly on the side of his head. When he knocked on the door and said he'd been riding for three days straight and needed some water, food, and a place to sleep – well, Jack, and Emile, and I all answered together. I had the shotgun, just in case. Where you coming from and where you going? Jack asked. This was when you still tried to help folks out you didn't know, because we were all still learning how to survive then, before we learned the real lesson that you survived by making sure that others didn't, because a dead man can't hurt you – but still we were learning – we knew to be suspicious. Nowhere, he said, just riding, and then he reached up, touched his own face in the night and his finger looked like bone, itself, like a skeleton, like Death himself had come to visit us at our door. You okay, mister? Jack asked. You don't look too good. Jack was always full of questions. Just tired, I've about ridden myself to death, the Rider replied. So I got him a jug of water and a stale loaf of bread and let him stay out in the back shed. You can tie your horse up outside, I said, just watch for the spiders out here. He drank the water straight away and just picked at the bread a little and then, without saying no word, he just went straight to bed like the soul just done left his body. I should've known something were wrong with him, how sweaty and pale he was, how come he'd stopped at such an out of the way place. I should've tried to figure what he was running from – but word travels slow now, we only hear it from folks who pass through, and there aren't many of those, so we didn't know about the plague yet.

Jack found him the next day, face covered in that scabby red mask of death, and he must not of tied his horse up right cause it had run away in the night, and so then it was Jack's idea also to burn the shed down, which I didn't like one bit because I helped my daddy build that shed with his own two hands, but he said the disease probably had it well near contaminated, so Jack made us tie scarves round our mouths and douse the thing in some of the little gasoline that we had left – but it worked cause the whole thing went up real high in a blaze, and the flames just exploded out so's we had to run back and within about ten minutes had covered the whole top of the shed and the flames looked like they were trying to climb up to heaven. We stayed by the fire pretty much the whole day, making sure to keep feeding it, so it burned everything out right and wouldn't die before it ate all it had to, but midway through, when we were looking at the fire, Jack disappeared and left us with his shotgun. But when he came back he had the two rifles we used to kill deer and gave them both to us, and that's when he said the thing that surprised us and was the first time I learned for sure what the world had become like after the event and all. Shoot anyone you see come near here, Jack said, and that's how Emile came to shoot Mr Jackson, our near neighbour about eight miles like down the road.

Jackson'd been stumbling and talking all strange, and Emile didn't even bother to talk to him but just shot him straightaways like Jack said, though Jack wasn't too happy at first, because he figured Emile should have known he'd just meant strangers, and that Jackson was probably just drunk and that was why he was stumbling, and who knew what kind of thing Jackson's sons were going to do, but it turned out to be a damned good thing, too, because when we got to 20 feet of him he was lying in the tall grass just near the edge of the clearing around our property, and we could see the red dots, the sores that marked his face, and we knew Jackson didn't have no sons to take revenge on us no more, and Jack told us to go back into the house.

But maybe though it was right for Emile to do that it was also a bad omen, too, because we had always been taught to love our neighbour and not just to shoot him down like some animal in the woods, which is what Emile kept saying cause even though he's always been the simple brother, Emile still feels things, and he was kind of crying and drinking some of the corn whisky Jack'd started making to trade to the Jacksons and others for more food, and Emile just kept saying how Jackson'd gone down just like a doe, his leg kind of twitching like slightly, but otherwise he'd just tumbled straight over, and so we gave him a bit more whisky and settled into the living room with our rifles and the candles out, taking turns on the lookout, and when I woke it was first light and Emile was shaking me cause Jack was unconscious, and he wasn't waking up. He had the fever now, and we didn't know what to do, so we took him up to the second floor in the cooler room and tried to keep a damp cloth on his forehead, but that didn't do no good, and though I told him to go to sleep, Emile sat up the whole night with Jack, holding him and wetting the cloth. But I went downstairs and decided to sleep, and when I woke again in the morning I walked up and Jack had the sores and Emile was holding him and rocking him back and forth, but I didn't even need to look real close cause I knew that the body weren't breathing – that that was it for Jack, and the fever had taken him and then the sores which was all were left of him, so I grabbed Emile's hand and pulled him out of the room right quick – Listen, Emile, now, listen, Jack's gone now, you understand, we gotta look out for each other now, okay, I'm gonna take care of you, okay? So I went and tried to do something with Jack's body, but then I just looked at his face, and I could see that even though he were dead the sores had gotten worse and that it hardly looked like Jack at all but that something had eaten him and then decided it didn't like the taste. It were my brother, but it were also death and I just about vomited and shit myself and pissed into the bargain, so I up and closed the door behind me, and said I would try my whole life to forget the red pocks all over his face, and that were all the eulogy and burial poor Jack ever got.

And I knowed for sure what to do next day when I saw Emile shaking, my own brother shaking, and he was shaking, a little pale, and I touched his forehead, and I could tell it was the fever, and so I did the only thing I could even though I had promised to take care of him, and so I said, C'mon Emile let's go, we got to do something, and he said, What are we doing? and I said, C'mon with me and you'll see, and he went to grab his rifle, but I told him no that was okay to leave it here cause I had mine and so we walked out past that burnt shed into the woods, and we went in about another 300 feet or so and when I stopped I could tell Emile looked at me, and I know it too that something come and changed in my eyes, and that he just knew, and he just said, No, oh my, no, oh for the love of God, no, but there weren't no one to hear him but me, and I didn't say nothing back cause how could I? He was my brother, and I was supposed to protect him, but I raised the rifle and did what I had to do, and it only took me one shot, and he went over. And I was sick at what I done. Sick to death, sick to death. But then it's only now when I look back on this I know it weren't the disease or the death that scared me so much as that after the event, and now with the sickness, that this was God telling me something, telling us all something – and that was that the disease weren't so much the thing that made us sick as it was that it was we who were the disease, we were the thing that done and infected everything – produced just like bacteria do – it was we that was the disease and the sickness was our cure and that if this were the plague wiped mankind off of the earth, truth was that it was probably all for the best, cause everything we ever up and done's all but a heap of ashes anyways, and there ain't ever been a thing we found that we ain't wanted to destroy or own or take, and our selfishness knows no bounds cause there's nothing we won't do to save ourselves, so it seems. And this made me feel a little better. Cause someday, when there won't be none of us left, someday when we been erased, then there won't be no one at all, and I liked that because that means there won't be anyone left to know what I done. No one to know the thing that I did to my own brother. And on that day when there ain't no humans left on the earth, then it'll be over. The sickness'll be gone and the healing can begin.

About the Contributors

Chelsea Avard
Chelsea Avard was born in Melbourne in 1977 and raised in Auckland, Sydney and Seramban, Malaysia. She trained as a classical dancer and now lives in Melbourne with her husband, Tim. She is in her second year of the Creative Writing PhD at the University of Adelaide and has been previously published in *The Body: An Anthology* and *The Sleepers Almanac*.

Gillian Britton
Gillian Britton studied speech pathology and music before developing a less-distracted interest in writing. She had a number of short stories published in the 1990s, and won the Unibooks Short Story Competition in 1997. In the ensuing time she has been raising children, earning money and working on numerous creative projects, including the slow formation of a novel. She lives on the further reaches of the Adelaide Hills (about the place where the rain and the hills peter out).

William Brown
William Brown has been attracted to the written word since he learnt to read. After a brief stint of writing, and editing poetry anthologies in high school, he studied english literature at Queen's University. Hailing from Canada, William is now studying Creative Writing at the University of Adelaide and hopes to make a career of it . . . writing, he means, not studying at uni.

Christy Di Frances

Christy Di Frances graduated *summa cum laude* in 2003 with a degree in English from Wisconsin Lutheran College, where she was the recipient of the annual Renaissance Award in English Literature. She also spent time studying fiction writing at Wheaton College in Illinois. She is currently working on her first novel while pursuing an MA in Creative Writing at the University of Adelaide.

Katherine Doube

Katherine Doube lost her passport on the Thailand–Laos border in 2004. She was most distressed. 'Walking the Thin Edge' is her first short story to be published. She is currently completing an MA in Creative Writing at the University of Adelaide.

Rebecca Ebert

Rebecca Ebert is currently completing her Creative Writing Honours at the University of Adelaide. She is a columnist with *The Barossa* and *Light Herald* and was published in the poetry anthology *Beyond Free: New poems in traditional metres*.

Susan Errington

Susan Errington was born in Adelaide. She is currently studying towards a PhD in Creative Writing at the University of Adelaide. Her first novel, *Olive Street*, was short-listed for the Victorian Premier's Literary Award for First Fiction, and has also been published in Holland as *Nacht in Olive Street*. Her short stories have appeared in *Smashed, Penguin Summer Short Stories 2* and *Spiny Babbler*. She was a winner of the 2002 University of Canberra Short Story Competition and was highly commended (writing under a pseudonym) in the 2002 *Melbourne Age* Short Story Competition.

Emilie Field

Emilie Field graduated with honours from Black Forest Academy, Germany, in 2003 and returned to Adelaide for tertiary study. She was the recipient of one of the University of Adelaide's Byard/Tormore Prizes for English I in 2004. She is currently pursuing a BA and a Diploma in French.

Petra Fromm

Petra Fromm spent her childhood travelling the world courtesy of the British Army. She now has three inspiring, grown-up children of her own. This leaves her time for more engaging pursuits – exploring concepts of identity for a PhD and drinking cheap red wine. Before returning to academia, she proofread other people's work (which creates ambiguous feelings in a would-be author). But on good days, she now considers herself a writer and is also collaborating on a fantasy novel with a young scientist. Petra hopes his research into alzheimer's progresses quickly, so that her old age harbours wealth and its associated eccentricities.

Doug Green

Doug Green is a cook by trade and specialises in recipes for disaster. He may be contacted at: black_hound_13@hotmail.com.

Rachel Hennessy

Rachel Hennessy completed her MA in Creative Writing at the University of Adelaide in 2004. Her MA manuscript 'The Quakers' was short-listed for the Varuna Writers' Centre Manuscript Development Award, long-listed for the 2005 *Australian*/Vogel Award and won the ArtsSA Creative Writing Award. She has been published in *The Body: An Anthology* and *Spiny Babbler*. She is currently pursuing her PhD in Creative Writing.

Blake Jessop

Blake Jessop studies writing at the University of Adelaide and is currently working on his first novel.

Stefan Laszczuk
Stefan Laszczuk was born in 1973. In 2005 he published his first novel, *The Goddamn Bus of Happiness*. In 2003 he published a book of short stories, *The New Cage*. In 2001 he had a letter published in the *Advertiser*. In 1999 he graffitied a toilet wall. In 1997 he wiped his snot on the seat at a bus stop. The list goes on, but believe me, you don't want to know about it.

Carol Lefevre
Carol Lefevre is an MA Creative Writing student at the University of Adelaide. She has published journalism and short stories in Australia and the UK and in July 2005 her first non-fiction writing was included in an anthology published by Granta.

Ilona Merckenschlager
Ilona Merckenschlager lives in a mud house on the Murrundi floodplains with Damian, Connor and Niamh.

Dena Pezet
Dena Pezet is a solicitor and barrister working in the financial services sector. She currently lives in Adelaide with her husband Nick and two dogs, Phoebe and Nipper. She is working on a novel, of which 'Scissors, Paper, Stone' is an extract.

Sim Ren
Sim Ren is a Malaysia-born writer who now resides in Australia. She is currently at the University of Adelaide, working on a novel entitled 'The Village of Wild Figs', and writing a PhD paper on childhood discourses in contemporary adult fiction. She is also interested in cross-cultural narratives, particularly in Sino- and Indo-English writing.

A M Sladdin
Poetry? Plays? Fine art? Long and short stories? Go ask Alice. For gallery appointment, call (08) 8847 4280.

Cassie Smith-Christmas

Cassie Smith-Christmas is a third-year student studying English and Linguistics. This is her second publication, the first being a short story published in *Winged Nation*, a gender-issues magazine. Her interests lie mainly in folktales and languages, and she has some crazy notion of combining the two loves by packing her bags and relocating to Ireland in the near future.

Anna Solding

Anna Solding has had stories published in *Forked Tongues*, *The Body: An Anthology* and *Cracker!* which she also helped edit. She loves a challenge and has therefore recently taken on the job as one of the Fiction editors of the new magazine *Wet Ink*. Her second manuscript is a novel of short stories that she is currently finalising. When she isn't writing or roaming the world presenting obscure papers, she enjoys hanging out with her gorgeous two-year-old son and her patient partner.

Rudi Soman

Rudi Soman was born in Singapore and spent the early part of his childhood in the USA. He has written for the *Weekend Australian* and the odd magazine. Recently Rudi has also been a scriptwriter for ABC Asia Pacific and worked on a series of SBS television mini-docs. He is currently writing his first novel.

Emmett Stinson

Emmett Stinson is working on his MA in Creative Writing at the University of Adelaide. He has won the *Melbourne Age* Short Story Award, the ArtsSA Creative Writing Award, and a Lannan Poetry Fellowship. He also serves as Fiction editor for *Wet Ink*, a new South Australian magazine of writing.

Heather Taylor Johnson

Heather Taylor Johnson is eagerly awaiting the PhD party she plans on throwing herself to celebrate the end of her two-and-a-half-decade stint as a professional student. She then wants to focus on bringing new lives into this world, both fictional and baby-soft real.

Lesley Williams

Lesley Williams is currently undertaking a PhD in Creative Writing. A life-interest in the earth, in aspects and evolutions of landscape, and in human interaction with the land, has led to an equally strong interest in aspects of language, story, culture and perceptions that infuse and impact on place. This in turn has become part of a long journey to explore, through memoir and narrative, dis/connections with un/familiar locations that could be called a re/cognition of home and a journey of be/longing.

Dominique Wilson

Dominique Wilson is completing her MA in Creative Writing at the University of Adelaide. Her work has appeared in *The Body: An Anthology* and UniSA's reader *Writing and Reading the Short Story – 1998*. Her short stories have been broadcast on Radio Adelaide. She is co-managing editor of the new magazine *Wet Ink*, and co-editor of this year's Australasian anthology *Spiny Babbler*.

Acknowledgements

The editors would like to thank Professor Nicholas Jose for his time and energy in making this year's anthology happen. We are grateful to the University of Adelaide and Michael Neale for supporting this project.

Thank you, also, to the staff of the Creative Writing program at the University of Adelaide – Dr Phillip Edmonds, Janet Harrow and Dr Susan Hosking – for their continuing hard work and inspiration.

Thank you to all the writers for contributing their literary babies.

Thank you to Rudi Soman for his ideas.

Thank you to all at Wakefield Press for their ongoing support.

Thank you to Simon Lownsborough for the cover design.

And a special thank you to Thomas Shapcott for getting the anthologies started in the first place and for always saying 'yes'.